The West Wolf

LANCE HOWARD

A Black Horse Western

ROBERT HALE · LONDON

© Howard Hopkins 2001
First published in Great Britain 2001

ISBN 0 7090 6792 5

Robert Hale Limited
Clerkenwell House
Clerkenwell Green
London EC1R 0HT

Typeset by
Derek Doyle & Associates, Liverpool.
Printed and bound in Great Britain by
Antony Rowe Limited, Wiltshire

J.T.

ONE

At the sound of approaching hoofbeats and a snapping shout Serene Hargrove's stomach plunged. Poised next to the cast-iron stove in the kitchen of the ranch house, she tensed. A shiver darted down her spine, despite the heat given off by the Franklin.

She set the heavy iron skillet on an unlit burner and, swallowing, edged around. Gaze lifting to the double windows, she forced herself to look out into the frosty moonlit night.

He is home . . .

The realization turned her insides to ice.

Another yell. Like the crack of that devil whip he always carried.

She saw him then. All but tumbling out of the saddle, he stumbled rubber-legged towards Clay Hargrove, his nephew, their only 'hand on the horse ranch. Her husband flung the reins at the younger man and took him to task for some unknown mistake.

Clay's face twisted into beaten lines, blue eyes focused on the ground, features flushed with embarrassment and fear. He nodded, walked off, leading the horse towards the livery.

Red-faced, Jothan Hargrove staggered towards the house.

She hurried back to the stove and scooped a thick beefsteak from the skillet, praying she had cooked it to his liking this time. Rare. Blood ran from the meat, puddling on the plate.

It does not matter. He will not like it.

He never approved of the way she did anything: how she cooked his meals, how she dressed or kept house, how she made love. Any display of tenderness on her part was something to be taken swift advantage of, smothered; any display of anger or defiance was something to be crushed, beaten from her.

The front door slammed and, dark eyes flinching, she bit her lower lip to keep it from quivering. She struggled to suppress the swelling dread, knowing it would spur him to prey on her vulnerability all the more. She was Apache, one of the *Diné*, and she begged herself to summon that strength, search deep inside and resist the dark beast of fear.

She stared at the doorway leading to the parlour, unseeing, steeling herself.

'What the galldamn hell you lookin' at through the winder, Injun?' a harsh voice lashed out and she jolted from her spell. His accusative tone cut through her like a winter wind.

Dark eyes searching the floor, she mumbled, 'Nothing, I . . .'

'Horse spit! You were lookin' at Clay again, weren't you? You got some sort of thing for that boy.'

'No, I was not.' Her voice wavered and she prayed to Ussen, the Giver of Life, Jothan would not take that as a sign of a lie. 'I merely heard a noise and looked to see what it was.'

He stepped deeper into the room, gait stuttering,

body swaying. Tossing his battered Stetson on to the hand-hewn table, he glared at her with bloodshot glazed eyes. 'You lyin' heathen, you galldamn look me in the eye when you talk to me!' She barely understood his slurred words and cursed him for drinking so much again. Whiskey always made things worse. Much worse. The more he drank the harder the beatings would be and tonight he appeared more in his cups than normal. She knew he had been with Clinton Hasley again. When they met, they met at the saloon and liquor flowed like a spring mountain river. Hasley bought the whiskey and his 'generosity' seemed unlimited. She wondered why Jothan did not realize the newspaperman used this to his own purpose. But Hasley's firewater would never get him whatever he sought. No matter how much Jothan drank, his secrets stayed locked within him. Instead he returned home and punished her more severely.

She forced her gaze to meet his. His blood-coloured eyes reflected hate, vile bitter fury at her, at the world, at everything. With a glimpse into the darkness that was Jothan Hargrove, she knew she was merely a focus for something he had been or done in the past. That darkness, discontent, unsatisfied with possessing him alone, unfurled onyx wings to encompass any other vulnerable to its dominion.

'You best have vittles on, Injun.' Spittle gathered at the corners of his mouth.

'It is ready.' Her voice came like the whisper of an Apache spirit on the wind.

'Why the Christamighty ain't it on the table, then?' His lips turned in a disapproving sneer.

'I am sorry. I did not realize what time you would return from town . . .'

'Well, that ain't no excuse. I'm powerful hungry now.'

She turned and hurried to the counter, scooping fried red potatoes and Hubbard squash into the plate beside the steak. She selected a fresh sourdough biscuit from a basket covered with a blue-checked cloth. She hesitated, nausea born of fear pushing into her throat. The aromas of sizzled meat and yeasty dough repulsed her, made her belly rebel because she had come to associate them so much with this time, when he stormed in drunk, demanding supper. As if familiar warm scents had become a portent of evil.

She brought the plate to the table, sliding it before him as he dragged back a hand-hewn chair and fell into it.

Jothan Hargrove jammed his elbow to the table and pressed a palm against his brow, as if he were having a hard time holding up his head.

'I'm sorry I treat ya bad, sometimes, Serene . . .' he whispered and she cringed.

Why did he apologize? Why did he let that ghost of guilt seep through his fury? It was a harbinger, she knew, like the coming of Winter Man, and it turned her insides to stone.

'It is not necessary to apologize,' was all she could say. She fought to keep all emotion out of her voice, but must have let something bleed through, because when he looked up at her a storm moved across his eyes.

Uncertain what was coming, she dared not speak. He reached into his pocket and plucked out a silver flask. Uncapping it, he took a deep pull. After, he swiped a forearm across his mouth and banged the flask on the table.

'Almost got that galldamn critter of yourn earlier today. Just missed the mangy thing.'

She lost the composure she had struggled so hard to maintain and fear mixed with defiance surged into her voice.

'He has done nothing to you! Please, do not hurt him.'

Darkness flashed in his eyes. 'Hell, galldamn prairie wolf boogers the horses and you damn well know it. What the hell is it with you Injuns, anyway? You worship them galldamn things?'

'He is coyote. He is . . . a pet.' Tears flooded her eyes and she struggled to keep them from flowing. Sooner or later he would kill the animal she had befriended, her attachment to her heritage. He had virtually wiped out all traces of her Apache culture, every distinction that made her one of The People, and the beast would be next.

Jothan surveyed her, watery eyes scanning her form as if inspecting her for betraying signs of the red that mingled with her white blood. He laid out her clothing every morning, demanding she wear the simple ging-ham dresses, forbidding her to place her raven hair in braids. He had buried the few trinkets she had come here with, allowing her to keep only the Plains-style moccasins because they tread softly when he awoke with his head throbbing from too much whiskey. Jothan Hargrove insisted her white half be the only part visible to the outside world, though it was impos-sible to conceal her dark hair, despite its auburn high-lights, and deep chocolate Apache eyes. She often wondered, in the deep hours of the night, when she dared not fall asleep for fear he would awake and take her, why he had chosen a bride who was of the *Diné*. What quirk of his darkness made him select a woman so obviously of mixed blood?

'He's a galldamn varmint and I'll get him one of these days, mark my words.'

'Do not kill him.' The words escaped before she could stop them, laced with defiance. She wondered what made her stand up to him when she knew it would only cause him to inflict more pain. But she could not help it. She was half Apache; it could not be strained from her blood like gold from stream water.

'You best not be tellin' me my business, Injun.' His eyes locked with hers and she fought the compulsion to step back, refusing to give in to fear. 'That beast is as good as buzzard food, I catch him comin' 'round here again. Hell, maybe I'll make you a right nice coat outta him. You Injun squaws like that, doncha?' He followed it with a mushy laugh that made her face surge with the heat of anger.

She wanted to shout she would kill him if he hurt that animal, wanted to scream she would put an Apache arrow straight through his black heart. But she couldn't. Because as she peered deep into his dark soul fear swallowed her, trembling through her body like a peyote death vision.

As if losing interest in taunting her. Jothan Hargrove grabbed a fork and knife, slicing off a huge slice of beefsteak and jamming it into his mouth.

For a spiteful moment she prayed he would choke on it.

On cue, as he lifted another hunk of steak to his lips, she took her place standing beside the table while he ate, two feet back, hands folded before her stomach. He never allowed her to sit with him, merely watch, in case he should need more food. She took her supper later, after he finished and fell into a liquor-drenched sleep. She preferred it that way. It was the only peace she got, though most of that time was spent with the fear he would awaken and demand to couple with her. As with every other aspect of his makeup, Jothan Hargrove was brutal lover, more savage than he accused her people of being.

Moments dragged by and she scarcely breathed. When at last he gazed up at her, she tensed visibly, unable to stop herself.

He smiled, the expression laced with bitter satisfaction. 'You go into town tomorrow. Fine stud horse due to arrive at the livery. Make sure you fetch it. An' make sure you ain't wearin' them galldamn moccasins, neither. Don't need you lookin' like no Injun whore.'

She searched for her voice. 'I will retrieve the horse.'

He gave a sharp nod. 'Damn right you will.'

Attention returning to his meal, he shoveled a forkful of squash into his mouth, instantly spitting it back out in yellowish globs that splattered the table. Anger lashing his eyes, he swiped a forearm across his mouth. 'What the devil's green hide is this slop, Injun?'

She flinched as if struck. Her heart began to pound again. 'It is Hubbard squash. It is in season.'

'Ain't no squash I ever et tasted like that.'

A wave of fear made her legs weak. Why hadn't she known better? She had made a stupid mistake in trying to please him, and now she would pay for it.

'I used Indian spice to flavour it. The yellow flesh is dry and tasteless without it.' Her voice shook.

His face darkened. 'Hell, how you expect me to eat this cowflop?' A burst of fury sizzled across his bloodshot eyes and his arm slashed out, sending the plate flying from the table. It bounced off a wall and food splattered across the papering and puncheon floor.

'I am sorry, I only meant to please you—'

'Galldammit, woman, you know better'n that!' He stood and grabbed the flask, gulping a pull. 'Reckon I'll just drink my supper, if'n it makes you no nevermind.'

He could drink himself to death for all she cared.

The thought must have bled on to her face, because his eyes narrowed and the uncomfortable bloated silence that always occurred before he let loose filled the kitchen.

He straightened and she edged back a step, trembling like a newborn calf. He gave her a smile like a wolf eyeing a fold.

He eased back the flap of his duster and ran his hand lovingly over the handle of a blacksnake coiled at his hip.

Panic seized her and she staggered another step backward. Her mouth moved in a silent plea for him not to do what he intended, but the wolf smile only intensified and viciousness glinted in his eyes.

He came towards her, seeming to grow in size with each step, until he overwhelmed all her senses and she was a-swim in a torrent of panic and fright.

'Please do not do this, Jothan.' Her voice was virtually nonexistent. 'Please . . . do not hurt me again . . .'

'You'll jest never learn, will ya, Injun? Your world no longer exists. It hasn't since the moment I rode into your camp and bought you from that no-good Injun headman of yourn for twenty pieces of horse flesh. You're nothin' more than squaw trash and that's all you'll ever be.'

'Why do you do this?' Her lips trembled. 'I have done nothing but try to please you.'

He backhanded her, a vicious swipe. She had no chance to avoid the blow and absorbed it full force. Pain rattled through her teeth and blood spurted from her mouth. Her legs buckled, but stubbornness kept her from falling, made her more determined to withstand his assault. Tears rushed from her eyes, streaming hot over her cheeks.

'You know better'n to backtalk me, you dumb squaw. You ain't no better than that critter out there. You gotta be trained, broken till you act the way you're galldamned s'posed to. I got big plans and I won't have no half-breed messin' 'em up. I been negotiatin' a big deal and it'll make me even richer than I am now, soon as Hasley comes 'round to my way of thinkin'. Galldamn gouger wanted fifty per cent, you believe that? What kinda fool does he take me for, anyhow?'

She glared at him through tears and pain. So that was it: Hasley wanted a bigger part of something than Jothan was willing to offer and they had haggled over it.

A mournful howl shattered the silence that followed. It ululated across the dusk like a death knell, and she saw the fury snap back into his eyes.

'Galldamn that critter!' He let out a string of curses that made her cringe as much as the threat of a blow. His hand rested on the handle of the blacksnake again and her eyes widened in terror.

'Oh, no . . .' she mumbled, shaking her head. His wolf smile grew more menacing and as he took another step towards her, she shrank back.

A roar burst from his lips and he grabbed her arm, fingers digging deep into the flesh. He swung her around and hurled her against the window. She hit hard, body shuddering with the impact. She expected the pane to shatter, to go plunging through into the night, her flesh sliced to ribbons, but the glass held.

His hand grabbed at her back, snatching up a handful of the gingham.

Oh, Spirit Above, please do not let this happen . . .

With a powerful yank, the cotton material and chemise beneath tore away, baring her back. As he continued pulling, the fabric came free of her front, exposing her breasts. He flung the cloth aside and shoved her forward, pressing her flesh to the chilled glass.

'Hell, you got such an all-fired interest in that no-good nephew of mine, let him see what he's gettin'!'

A flush of humiliation reddened her cheeks and she let out a small cry when she saw Clay coming back from the stable, gazing up, seeing her nakedness. The ranchhand quickly averted his eyes, fear and shock turning his face. Through her shame, she knew the young man respected her enough not to look, but knew as well he was too frightened of Jothan to help her.

Steeling herself for the first blow, she stared straight ahead into the gathering dusk, face emptying of emotion. She would beg for mercy no more; she would not give him that satisfaction.

The blacksnake cracked with the sound of a shot. Its flayed end sizzled across her back, leaving a blistering welt. Pain lashed deep into her flesh. She clamped her teeth together, refusing to utter a sound. If she cried out he would punish her worse. Weakness infuriated him.

'You best learn your lesson this time, Injun. I'm gettin' right sick of tryin' to civilize ya.'

You go to your white man's hell, Jothan Hargrove.

Turning her head, she pressed her cheek against the glass. Her eyes fluttered shut, a chant to ease the pain rising in her mind, shutting out the sound of his voice.

Then it was over. Her flesh would carry three more scars when the angry welts subsided.

She wasn't sure how much time passed, but when she dared to turn around he was gone and she stood alone in the kitchen. The blacksnake lay coiled on the floor, a serpent of fear that reminded her her life would never be her own as long as Jothan Hargrove walked the earth.

Outside, night had come, bringing an Apache moon and cleansing mist. A howl rose up, mournful and forlorn and she shuddered. Wrapping her arms about herself to cover her nakedness, she slumped to the floor beneath the window, tears rushing from her eyes until she could cry no more.

Dragging a rifle by its barrel, Jothan Hargrove staggered from the house. Head whirling from rotgut whiskey, a soft buzzing seemed to permeate all his thoughts. His heart pounded in mushy rhythm from the alcohol ossifying his system and a sheeny film of sweat glazed his forehead, despite the brisk snap of the late October night air.

Squinting, vision hazy, he surveyed the grounds. The moon was frosty, bloated like a pregnant cow tit and bright. It stung his bloodshot eyes and trimmed the grounds with interlocking ribbons of shadow and alabaster.

An errant chill wandered through him. Nothing born of cold, but of something else, an augur of menace for no reason he could reckon. Perspiration evaporated from his face in a chilled wave and he fought an impulse to go back into the house and fall asleep in his cups for the night.

Wasn't like him to be boogered for no reason. He controlled this spread the way he controlled that galldamn half-breed squaw he'd left in the kitchen.

A twinge of guilt stabbed his innards, a sliver of regret, and he almost felt sorry he had whipped her that hard. What the hell was wrong with her, anyway? Why couldn't she ever get anything right, and why was she so galldamned attached to that prairie wolf he'd spent half the mornin' tracking?

The glimmer of compunction died and he cursed, spat. Hell, she deserved what she got. How else was he to train the savage out of her?

He probed in a pocket and brought out the flask he

had taken from the table. Pulling off the cap, he swallowed a slug. Rotgut burned its way down his gullet, nestling warm in his belly, providing him with a surge of courage.

A howl came, eerie, moaning, ululating on the brittle wind. Was there something different about it? Didn't sound quite right to his ears, and the direction seemed different than earlier. Shaking his head, he let the notion pass. Whatever the case, the critter was close. Damn prairie wolves came nearer at night, though he hoped to track and kill it during the day when it was most vulnerable.

Why did he want it dead so all-fired bad? The mangy thing really hadn't caused any damage and never got near the horses, as he claimed it did. Because Serene was attached to it, showed it the love and affection she would never show him. He deserved that devotion and respect, not some galldamned animal.

A horse neighed and he gazed in the direction of the stable. He listened, noting an element of nervousness in the animal's tone.

Hell and tarnation, maybe things had finally gone his way. Maybe that mangy pest was after the stock after all.

A low growl reached his ears and he froze, the courage granted by rotgut dissolving.

'Galldamn,' he muttered, running his tongue over dry lips and clenching the Winchester more tightly.

Something was wrong.

What?

Was it the fact the coyote had never bothered the horses until tonight? That the growl sounded somehow different, more throaty and less rounded than a normal prairie wolf's? Or was it something else, some dark awareness that promised him the cruelty he showed Serene was going to come around and bite him in the britches sooner or later?

Perhaps it was something more tangible. Hasley? Something about that fella and his mental defective kin wasn't right, though hell and tarnation the scalawag put up a good front. Jothan Hargrove recognized fronts all too well. He knew when that Injun woman was hidin' her fear from him to avoid bein' beaten worse, and he knew when Clinton Hasley was trying to sheep-dip him in negotiating their deal. That's why all the whiskey in Wolf's Bend wouldn't pull the secret of where things were hidden out of him. Hasley had another think comin' if he figured that was the case. Hell, that ink mule was a rank amateur compared to him and his past associations.

Whatever the case, Jothan Hargrove was experiencing something he hadn't felt since dealing with that stage-robbin' gang leader from his past – fear. He wondered if this was the way Serene felt when he whipped her, but quickly dismissed the notion. Course not. Injuns didn't feel. They were savages. every last one of 'em.

Lifting the Winchester and tucking the stock beneath an arm, Hargrove stepped from the porch and walked towards the stable.

A spider-web mist carpeted the landscape. Glazed with silvery strands of moonlight, it twirled and shimmered like ghosts cavorting. Suppressing a shiver, he paused, gaze locking on the building where he boarded his prize horseflesh.

A low growl invaded his woolgathering and his gaze narrowed. The stable rose up from the gauzy mist, marbled with shadow and alabaster. He cursed himself for being boogered. It was only a galldamn building. It never seemed threatening before. Yet somehow it was now, made more so by the fact that both doors gaped open, the entrance a maw of blackness.

'Galldammit, Clay. I'll beat your britches for this,' he muttered, brow knotting. He cursed that no-good nephew of his for leaving those doors open again. Where the hell had he gotten off to, anyway? He had already peeled his rattle earlier for forgetting to mend the corral.

'Clay?' he yelled, tugging the flask from his pocket and swallowing another bolt of courage. 'Clay, where the galldamn hell are you?'

Silence. He swore he heard the mist whispering, but it was only the breeze rustling through the brittle fall leaves.

He tucked the flask back into his pocket and wiped his mouth on a sleeve. Gathering his nerve, he took tentative steps forward. He thrust the Winchester out in front of him. 'I'll get you this time, you mangy critter. You'll make a galldamn fine coat.'

A sharp howl rang out from inside the stable and he jolted, stopping in his tracks. The sound scared a mess of years off his life, he reckoned.

Something's wrong.

Again the notion struck him. That howl ... that coyote didn't sound that way. Something about it was peculiar, less animal-like than it normally was. Maybe the beast had come down with the foam and that's why it was boogerin' the horses. That would explain the throatier growl, too.

Hell, in that case that ungrateful squaw would kiss his boots for doin' her a favour by savin' her life from a diseased animal. Everyone knew if'n you got yourself bit by a sick critter you died a horrible death.

A nervous laugh escaped his lips. He levered a shell into the chamber and went forward. A sick animal made an easy target.

Stopping at the entrance, he peered inside. The interior pregnant with gloom, patches of moonlight seemed in motion, chasing shadows.

'Where the hell are you, you flea-bitten mutt?' The words came with far less force than he intended.

A horse neighed and another joined in chorus behind it. He heard them shuffle in their stalls, spooked by something he couldn't see.

Jothan took a step into the stable, a warm slithery feeling flowing over him.

The growl sounded again, low and menacing, and he stopped dead. It dawned on him the growl didn't really sound like that of a sick animal. It carried no liquid quality, no high-pitched edge of pain or distress, as he had heard from other afflicted beasts.

Eyes adjusting somewhat to the gloom, narrowing, he tried to spot the coyote, finding it impossible to pick out more than the larger dark shapes of stalls and hay bales, the shadowy heads of horses.

Something moved with a flurry of motion just to his right. He made out a hairy shape that appeared far larger than a coyote. Reflexively, he jerked the Winchester's trigger, loosing a roaring blast that shuddered his entire body and shattered his composure. Lead ploughed into a floorboard with a *chunk!* and the acrid odour of gunsmoke assailed his nostrils.

'Galldammit all to hell!' he blurted, knowing he might damn well have killed one of the horses, firing out of panic that way.

'Come on, you mangy sonofabitch, get your hide out here where I can see ya!' His voice reverberated in hollow echoes throughout the stable.

He listened, alert for any slight sound that would betray where the animal was located.

His eyes stopped, widened. An icy wave washed over

him. There! Just off to the left, a crouched shape—

'Judas Priest . . .' he muttered, words strangling in his throat. His hands began to quake and the Winchester jittered. Roughly ten feet away, the thing straightened from its crouch, rising on two legs, taller than any galldamned coyote ever was. Before he could make out what it was, it darted into the shadows.

'What the hell are you—'

A flash of movement. The thing lunged and he let out a bleat. With shaking hands he fought to get the rifle level and jerk the Winchester's trigger a second time.

Flame and smoke belched from the barrel, momentarily illuminating the shadowy contours of the creature leaping upon him. He let out a screech filled with terror. Now he knew how Serene felt when he beat her, knew the utter helplessness and surrender that paralyzed her soul. If he could have begged his Maker for redemption at that moment he would have fallen to his knees and babbled supplications seven ways to Sunday, but as surely as he now realized the wages of sin, he knew no salvation or mercy existed for a man such as he.

Hurried, the shot missed, bullet tearing splinters from a stall door.

The beast crashed into him with tremendous force, hurling Jothan backwards and down. His back slammed into the floor, breath knocked from his lungs. The creature came down atop him, pinning him to the boards. A vague musky odour pervaded the thing, along with the sour bouquet of old sweat and leather. The growl came again, imbued with maddened urgency and bloodlust.

Realizing he'd retained his grip on the Winchester, he struck out, trying to smash the thing's hairy skull. The creature jerked its head sideways, reflexes incredibly swift. The stock went sailing over its shoulder and Jothan lost his grip on the rifle. It clattered on the floorboards ten feet away.

Jothan's own reflexes weren't quite as fast. He saw the great furry hand jerk backwards and up, come shrieking down in a vicious arc, but could not get his head out of the way. Welts of pain slashed across his face as razor-sharp claws shredded the flesh clear to the bone. Blood streamed down his cheek and puddled on the boards and he began to blubber with terror.

A clubbing paw slammed into his temple, sending explosions of light across his vision. He lay there, stunned, staring up at the creature as it jerked its taloned hand upward and struck again and again and again.

Flesh tore in great flaps from his face and chest. Clothes shredded and the thing let out an ear-splitting howl of victory. His vision clouded with crimson and tears.

The events of the night streamed through his mind and he saw Serene's face, saw himself bringing the blacksnake down and it melded into one image with the striking beast's clawed hand.

The furred hand rose a final time, poised for the finishing blow, momentarily caught in the moon's glow, vicious claws gleaming.

As it streaked downward, Jothan Hargrove closed his eyes and prepared to meet the Devil.

TWO

Tom Hogan slapped the dove on her rump as she climbed out of the bed. 'Get the hell out of here, Lulu Belle.'

The dove turned, casting him a perturbed glare as she tugged on her undergarments then slipped into her high skirt and peek-a-boo blouse. Hell, she wasn't the best looking whore he'd been with, but she did have a plumb ripe form and was fleshly in all the womanly places.

Lulu Belle fluffed her large ringlets of red hair and scowled. 'Why, that ain't no way to treat a lady, Mr Tom. I rung your bells right fine, I did.'

'Well, Jesus H. Christmas, Lulu Belle, if you show me a lady I might treat her like one!' He swung his legs out of bed and yanked on his red union suit and trousers. As he turned away from her in some strange quirk of modesty, he heard her laugh like a braying mule. The expression fitted her face better than he would have told her.

'What the hell's so all-fired funny?' He turned, jamming his hands to his hips.

Lulu Belle's eyelids fluttered in mock coyness. 'Why,

22

Mr Tom, you do pick the strangest moments to be struck shy.'

His brow scrunched. He gave her the once over, noting she looked a hell of a lot less attractive than she had an hour before when he was randy enough to walk bowlegged. She had a mulish face, a nose too large for the rest of her features and glassy green eyes that showed evidence of too much belladonna, which women in her profession used to ward off the pain of too-tight corsets and grew to abuse.

A shadow crossed his mood and he cocked an eyebrow. 'What's it matter to you? This is all you need worry about.' He plucked a double eagle from his pocket and flipped it to her. She caught it like a tinhorn catching a lucky streak.

Staring at the gold piece, green eyes gleaming, she giggled something that was almost pure. 'Why, Mr Tom, this is right generous of you. You could have me a week for this much.'

'Don't need you a week, Lulu Belle. After the turn you gave me tonight reckon I'd never survive it.' He gave her a smile that had little heart in it. Fact was, now that he was done with her, he just wanted her to leave him be. She was like looking into a mirror and what he saw staring back made him a hell of a lot more uncomfortable than he would have liked.

She batted her eyes. 'Why, honeybun, you ain't just whistlin' Dixie. When a fella gets in Lulu Belle's saddle he's in for the smoothest ride of his life.'

'Get the hell out – now.' His tone grew harsh as his mood darkened.

She threw him a look that said she was damned puzzled at his behaviour, but twenty in gold bought a lot of understanding, so she let it be.

She sighed with all the flourish of a steam engine

whistle blowing. 'You get a hankerin' for Lulu Belle again, Mr Tom, you send the hotel man a-callin'. I'll always make time for a gent like you.'

He turned to gaze out the dusty window, arms folded, insides churning with bitter condemnation at his own failings. 'Reckon I won't be needin' your services again, Miss Lulu Belle. Next time I'll find me a prettier whore.' He turned back to her and went to the door, opening it and offering her the trail. 'Git!'

'You're a hard man, Mr Tom.' Her kohl-tinted green eyes flamed but she kept most of the anger from her tone, likely not wanting to kill any chance of future business from a man who paid in such generous portions.

'You ain't the first to notice, Lulu Belle, an' you ain't likely to be the last.'

She harumphed and whirled on a high-laced boot-toe, then stalked out of the room. He watched her stomp down the cidery-lit hallway with all the grace of a drunken donkey.

Easing the door shut, he let out a weary breath. Back pressed to the door, his bitter blue eyes glazed with the detached lost look of a man who had left himself too far back in his past to ever saddle his future.

'You're a sonofabitch, you know that?' Hell, he hadn't needed to treat Lulu Belle that way, no matter how much he overpaid her. The double eagle for a dollar-a-favour whore was merely to alleviate his own guilt, and she deserved better.

With the guilt another feeling took hold, a biting ache of lonesomeness that overwhelmed him in weak moments, when he let his guard down, let himself be human.

Human?

He had a hell of a lot of nerve calling himself that, didn't he?

He pulled a worn silver flask from his pocket. Uncapping it, he drank deep of the Orchard within, letting it ease down his throat and chase away some of the shadows darkening his soul.

After another swallow, he tucked the flask back into his pocket and gazed about the dingy hotel room that held a sagging bed, a battered table, a rickety nightstand atop which sat a low-turned lantern, and a bureau holding a porcelain wash basin and pitcher.

He pushed himself away from the door and went to the bureau, splashing water from the basin into his face and toweling off. Elbows jammed to the bureau top, he placed his head in his hands, wandering through the inky mists of his torment.

You killed her . . .

He shuddered with a dark memory, struggling to force it away before it devoured him.

A sudden violent sweep of his arm sent the basin and pitcher flying across the room. The pitcher shattered against the wall, fragments raining to the floor. The basin splashed water across the threadbare print carpet and wobbled to stillness beside the bed.

Flinging himself away from the bureau, he went to the bedpost and grabbed his gunbelt, buckling it around his waist. He slid his Peacemaker from its worn holster and checked its load, an old habit, but one that gave him a measure of comfort.

For Tom Hogan lived by the gun. He lived by the lead that had ruined his soul. He tracked down hardcases and exacted justice, redemption by bullet or by hanging, without mercy and remorse. A manhunter. A paid killer. An avenger who used killing the guilty like a salve.

How many times do you have to pay for it, Hogan?
How many righteous acts does it take to cleanse a man's
soul?

He swallowed against the emotion lodged in his
throat and, grabbing his hat from a bedpost, went to
the door, opening it. Stepping out into a dingy hall of
blue-foiled papering and cidery lantern light, he went
to the stairs, descending.

Placing his Stetson atop a head of tousled brown
hair, he nodded at the hotel man, walked outside and
paused on the boardwalk.

A full moon gleamed high in a sky of indigo velvet,
glazing the wide, rutted main street with milky light.

Wolf's Bend had changed a good measure since he
lived here, better than twenty years past. He recollected it was a peaceful happy town, at least it seemed
such to an eighteen-year-old boy with a gleam of
justice in his eye and an ache for adventure in his
soul. A pristine raw settlement then, Wolf's Bend blos-
somed like a wilderness flower as prospectors and
speculators struck silver and gold in the nearby mountains and Colorado countryside. Riches flooded the
town's veins with abundance and Wolf's Bend sprang
up in the blink of an eye. Businesses flourished.
Families homesteaded parcels of land and build themselves a life. He recollected his own family had been
one of them.

The mining boom brought with it the usual under-
side of prosperity, frock-coated lawyers with more
avarice than scruples, gaudy-vested tinhorns, hoisted-
bosomed whores and glib-tongued grifters whose skill
at hornswoggling far outweighed any sense of moral
fortitude. It went hand in glove, but the law held a firm
grip that kept the graft and seamier aspect of wealth
under tight rein. Families prospered and sinners found

swift redemption during Sunday morning service at
the Methodist church two blocks over.

All that had changed and Tom bet the church could-
n't have held all the iniquity he saw carousing the
moon-splashed street tonight. With the sunfall, a
rowdy hullabaloo held sway. 'Hands from the local
ranches and mine workers staggered along the boardwalks towards the saloon, outside of which Kewpi doll-
painted women with coral-daubed cheeks and kohl-
tinted eyes stood against the wall, offering coy smiles
and flashes of flesh with the promise of wanton
delights bought and paid for. Drunks collapsed in the
street, snoring loud enough to rattle hanging signs,
fortunate if they didn't get trampled by horses or run
over by buckboards.

Whoops and yips, occasional gunshots punctuated
the brisk night air.

Tom shook his head and went towards the saloon,
boots clomping hollowly on worn dusty boards. Things
had changed but he reckoned he had little right to
condemn. He couldn't say what he expected to find
coming back to this place after twenty years, but something about it unnerved him, made him wish he had
the good sense to just saddle his horse and ride back on
out.

Upon reaching the saloon, he stepped through the
batwings.

Durham smoke clouded the barroom and the scents
of old booze, sweat and too liberally applied perfume
assailed his nostrils. Men cloistered around green-felt-
covered tables, dealing poker, cussing or yowling as
hands were either won or lost. Whores wearing peek-
aboo blouses or sateen bodices draped themselves over
winners' arms, creamy bosoms threatening to spill free
and offered for a share of a fella's good fortune.

A fight erupted as one fella called another a lowdown cheatin' piece of cowflop and slammed down his cards, throwing a vicious punch in nearly the same move. The second man made a play for his gun, but the barkeep leaped from behind the counter and popped him in the back of the skull with a scatter-gun. The offender hit the floor in a cloud of old sawdust and likely a life was saved. Two men dragged the unconscious card cheater past Tom and out through the batwings.

With a sigh, he threaded his way through the tables to the polished bar and settled on a stool. The place was pretty much as he recollected it, with the notable exceptions of the doves and fights. The bar took up most of the right side; hutches filled with booze lined the wall behind it, a large gild-framed mirror between them. The walls were papered in dull red stripes, adorned with paintings of buxomy nudes with old-fashioned curves. At the back a stairway led to an upper level; a door led to a storeroom and back hallway.

Tom's gaze settled on the 'keep, who was making a show of wiping off his hands as he ambled his way back behind the bar. The bartender was built along the lines of a pickle barrel with thick arms and sausagelike fingers. Tufts of white hair stuck out to either side of a balding pate. A long white beard dangled from his chin and a soup-strainer moustache nearly covered his lips. While the fellow had a pleasant face, a contrasting surly expression gave Tom the impression of an ornery Santa Claus.

'You always poleax your customers that way, Jeb?' Tom asked, forcing a lilt into his voice.

The 'keep cast him a surly eye. 'Why, Tom Hogan, you loathsome sonofabitch!' He slapped both hands on the bartop then reached beneath and pulled out a bottle of whiskey of much richer colour than the bottles nestled in the hutch.

Tom set his Stetson on the next stool. 'You got that right, you old sidewinder! Still watering the whiskey, I see.'

The 'keep slid a grin from ear to ear. 'You bet your britches I am. Hell, wouldn't make me an even livin' if'n I didn't.'

Tom cocked an eye. 'Pshaw! You can't fool me. How much you take out of the whores you send through the hotel man, anyway?'

'Knew I should've taken a switch to your backside a hell of a lot more often when I was raisin' ya. Might've taught you some respect for your elders.'

'Reckon it would have just made me more ornery.'

The 'keep poured a whiskey and slid it to Tom, who took a gulp, savouring the fiery liquor as it wandered down his gullet to warm his belly. Seemed like he could never rightly get enough of the redeye these days. It took more and more to take the edge off the guilt, chase away the nightmares.

The barman's face turned serious. 'Where the hell you been for twenty years, Tom? I've missed ya. You was like a gawddamn son to me and just ridin' off after, well, after what happened gave me a hell of a turn.'

Jim felt a stab of guilt. He'd never told Jeb he was riding out, never said good-bye, and looking back he could see it was damned inconsiderate of him.

'Reckon I just lost track of time, Jeb. Happens to manhunters on the trail.'

Jeb shook his head, tufts of white hair and beard jiggling. 'Hell it does. You made a mistake, son. Nothin' could have prevented what happened that day. It's the way of the West and sometimes innocent folk get killed. Runnin' from it don't change it none.'

Tom shifted on the stool, emotion choking him. 'I never should have got so full of myself. I didn't have a lick of experience and was just too all-fired cocky. Wasn't ready for split-second decisions.'

The 'keep braced both hands on the bartop, brow crinkling. 'You're beatin' yourself too much, son. The mistakes of youth ain't meant to last forever.'

Jeb's words got under his skin for no reason he could figure. 'What the hell would you know about it? You ain't the one who's got blood on your hands.'

Jeb held his ground. 'So you just keep on addin' more blood? That make it better, get rid of the ache in your soul?'

'Reckon it has to eventually.' He stared at his whiskey as he swirled it around in the glass.

'You know better'n that. You best recollect I been on this earth a hell of a lot longer than you have. I seen innocent men and women killed for no reason other than bein' in the wrong spot at the wrong time and I seen God take 'em on nothin' more than a whim. It ain't fair, but it's life and you ain't got a right to live yours so plumb full of guilt it poisons your soul.'

'Don't I? Seems I got every right.' He found it impossible to keep the bitterness out of his tone.

'Hell you do! I got nothin' against what you do, son. Lordamighty knows the West needs manhunters, least of your kind. Just don't you do it for the wrong reasons. Do it a-cause you believe in it, not a-cause you got some high-falutin' notion it will wipe your slate clean.'

Tom knew there was no arguing with the older man and settled for flippancy. 'Hell, twenty years later is a little late to be sellin' me that kind of snake oil, ain't it, Jeb?'

The barman's face took on an expression that said he would have none of Tom Hogan's lip. 'Don't you sass me, son. You didn't stick around long enough for me to give you advice before and now I figure I got lots of catchin' up to do.'

Relaxing, Tom let out an easy laugh. 'Reckon you do at that . . .' He threw a backward glance at the barroom, surveying the rowdy crowd and doves. Jeb Farley had run the Rusty Spur saloon since Tom was old enough to piss standin' up. While it had always catered to a lively sporting crowd it was certainly a hell of a lot more raucous now. The whores were new, too. Jeb was a cousin on his mother's side, a black sheep of sorts who had opened this 'parlour of iniquity', as his ma used to call it, when the Hogan family first came to Wolf's Bend on a hope and a prayer to strike their fortune. Tom's father was a rough and ready silverman of the old school and claimed himself a mine that panned out with some of the purest ore a prospector could imagine. He'd made that dream reality – until half a mine fell on him and sent Jacob Hogan to meet his Maker. His ma, always a sickly sort, had been given to spasmodic coughing fits since leaving Virginia to travel West, but after Jacob died her condition rapidly deteriorated until each spell came with increasing violence. It wasn't long after that a five-year-old boy stood before an open grave, crying and wondering why God Above had taken both his parents. Tom recollected Jeb guiding him from the cemetery, bringing him to the saloon and providing him with a room upstairs. For a black sheep, Jeb had done the best he could raising him, attempting to teach him right and wrong, pointing out the difference even when he abided with it in his saloon. Tom managed to grow up with a measure of innocence, despite his surroundings.

Until that day.

After that everything changed.

Coming from his reverie, his gaze focused on the 'keep again. 'What the hell happened to this town, Jeb? Never used to be this rowdy. Even your saloon's changed. You never had whores.'

'Your turn to lecture me now, eh, son?' The 'keep gave him that surly Santa look.

Tom grinned. 'Didn't think I'd miss an opportunity to give it back, did ya?'

Jeb slapped the countertop. 'Hell, you're too much like your ma, son. Just don't follow it up with a sermon to boot.'

'Reckon I ain't one to be preachin', Jeb. Not with what I got in my saddle-bags.'

The 'keep studied him. 'Ahh, now I know why Lulu Belle got sent for.'

Tom's face flushed with heat and he tried to cover it with a flip tone. 'Hell of a gal.'

'You're lucky she didn't steal you blind. Where the devil'd she get off to, anyhow?'

Tom's brow bunched and a flash of dread spiked through him for no reason he could figure. Perhaps it was his manhunter sixth sense dogging him. Perhaps it was nothing. Whatever the case, he wasn't a whore's keeper.

'She ain't here? I sent her away over an hour ago.'

'Knowin' Lulu Belle she took any money you gave her and headed like an Injun's arrow to stock herself up on belladonna.'

Tom shook his head. 'This town really has gone to hell in a handbasket, hasn't it?'

'Reckon some might say that, but I just change with the times. Men on the randy need a good woman now and then, even if she's bought and paid for. Didn't have me a boy to raise no longer, so I didn't have to set no examples. Town grew and its needs grew with it.'

'Grew or turned into a pig wallow?'

'Depends on whether you see the bottle half empty or half full. Me, I see the full side – opportunity.'

'That how it went? Mines made folks rich enough to buy all the vices they wanted?'

The 'keep bellowed a laugh and his beard quivered. 'Prosperity's a lovely lady, son. Curvy in all the right places and willin' in all the rest.'

Tom studied the older man, pondering. Despite Jeb's jocular demeanour a hitch rode his voice. 'You sound like you're frettin' on that lady goin' sundown on you.'

The 'tender nodded. 'Reckon I am a bit. See, since them killin's started folks are gettin' antsy. Ain't affected business much yet, but it keeps up it shore will.'

Tom's eyes narrowed, the dread he'd felt a moment ago strengthening. 'Killin's?'

The bartender's face set in grim lines. 'Yep, lost me three gals already, plus the Hargrove woman lost her husband. The sheriff got his, to boot.'

'Outlaws?'

'Wish it were that, son. Might make things a whole lot less fearsome, but it was something else, something horrible, like an animal attack, only not.'

'What's that s'posed to mean?'

'Only that whatever it was tore 'em up somethin' awful-like. Couldn't hardly tell who they was by the time that thing was finished. Makes goin' out at night a thinkin' proposition for some folks, 'specially on full moon nights when these killin's tend to take place.'

'Don't look like too many of 'em took it to heart, judgin' from the carousers out on the street and in here.'

'Well, like I said, they're just startin' to get antsy about it. But many a decent folk are stayin' in after nightfall.'

Tom's brow crinkled and he leaned back, running a finger over his lower lip. 'How you reckon some kind of animal could kill a sheriff with a gun?'

The 'keep shifted feet, gaze dropping, coming back up. 'Reckon maybe it wasn't all animal.'

'What the hell you mean, it wasn't all animal? It's either an animal or a man.'

'Well, them girls looked like they got torn up by a mountain lion or somethin', their faces plumb ripped off. Only animals don't usually kill just to kill. They kill for food or to defend their young'uns, but these deaths wasn't like that. Those gals looked like they was meant to be killed, same with the Hargrove fella and lawdog. Don't know no animal that particular.'

'Jesus H. Christmas, Jeb, you ain't serious? Gotta be a mountain cat or wolf of some sort. Likely a sick one.'

'That was the thinkin'. Some fellas even organized huntin' parties to go after it, but they never found any animal tracks near the body. None of the local ranches has reported cat or wolf attacks on any of their stock, neither. Plumb strange.'

'Hell, Jeb, you're startin' to sound like you're aimin' at spooks.'

The look on the 'keep's face shaded darker and he sighed. 'You saw what was left of those gals you might aim at a few yourself. That's why I was wonderin' where Lulu Belle got off to.'

'Whores can take care of themselves, Jeb.'

The 'keep frowned, giving him a disapproving look. 'Hell, son, you changed a mite, haven't you?'

'Don't follow.'

'You used to care 'bout folks, even the lowly types. That's what set you on the trail to bein' a manhunter in the first place.'

Another stab of guilt. He wished he could force the

feeling away. 'Reckon circumstance changes a fella, Jeb. Sometimes life shows him a darker side and there's no turnin' back.'

'You've seen that darker side more than most, doin' what you do, but it don't mean you gotta let it take away your compassion.'

'Don't it? What the goddamn hell does compassion have to do with anything in this life? No one showed that lady compassion twenty years ago.'

Jeb gave him a stern glare. 'Soften that attitude, son. I ain't about to let you backtalk me. Never did and won't now that you're a famous manhunter. Reckon it's your life and how you live it is your business, but runnin' off the way you did without a word was a downright sorry way to treat a father an' if we get down to brass tacks that's what I considered myself to be to you, least in all the ways I could be. For that you at least owe me a listen. You take a look in the mirror and search real hard, son. Somewhere under that face you got on against the world is that boy I knew and that boy cared about folks.'

Tom shifted, swallowed. 'Twenty years is a long spell, Jeb. Folks change.'

The barman eyed him and Tom wanted to squirm in his seat. Something inside him felt like an eighteen-year-old boy gettin' a whupping for stealing a fresh-baked apple pie from a neighbour's window sill. 'Then why the hell you back after all this time, son?'

'Don't know and don't give a damn.' He knew he had answered too fast.

The 'keep let out a disgusted sigh. 'You came back to face the ghosts, son. You came back to look inside and finally chase them away.'

'Don't reckon you're right, Jeb. I just came back to visit an a old friend and say howdy do.' He said it with biting flippancy but knew Jeb wasn't fooled. Hell, he didn't believe it himself.

Why did you come back?

Damned if he knew, but a twinge of discomfort made him afraid Jeb had hit the peg on the head.

The batwings swung open with a creak and Tom was relieved for the interruption. A man walked through, pausing just inside the doors. Tom's head swivelled in that direction as a blast of cold air hit his back. A ripple of that manhunter's sixth sense went through him as he watched the fellow stagger to a stool at the opposite end of the bar and collapse on to a seat. The 'keep grunted, ducked his chin at a dove, who went to the man, fetching him a whiskey.

He studied the fellow, unable to shake the warning bell ringing in his mind. A thick sloping brow and a nose that shown evidence of having been broken numerous times, small hard eyes and a blocky chin, nailed the fellow as a hardcase. Yet something else about him seemed vaguely askew and it took Tom a moment to place it. The hardcase had the look of a simpleton; his gaze wandered aimlessly, appearing distant, as if he weren't quite in his own head, some-how, but off somewhere else. Dressed in a grimy shirt and ragged trousers, he had a large frame, wide across the shoulders and thick in the biceps and legs. His hands were filthy, fingernails jagged and long, encrusted with dirt. An odd bulging scar snaked along his left temple.

'Local hardcase, or imported?' Tom nudged his head slightly in the man's direction.

'You might call him local, least for the past year or so. Lucas Hasley, brother of the newspaper owner, Clinton Hasley. He's kind of a half-wit, but he's got himself a mean temper and I've thrown his sorry britches outta here a few times. Got a bad habit of manhandlin' the gals, too. Used to get into lots of fights till he beat the hell out most of the competition. Strong as a gawddamn longhorn.'

'What do you mean by half-wit?'

'Slower than a churn-headed horse. In his younger days he hired on to some cattle outfit in New Mex. Got himself into a fix with some Apache warrior over a squaw and ended up with an arrowhead lodged in his brain for his troubles. Big piece of it still in there, too. That's why he's got that lumpy scar. Doc couldn't get it all out, but the sonofabitch lived through it and ever since he ain't right in the think box.'

'Anything other than fights or manhandling?'

'Nothin' I know about. He's got a powerful hate for Injuns, though, that's for sure. That Hargrove fella I told you got killed, well, he had himself this half-breed wife who still owns a spread a bit out of town. Lucas's always spoutin' off 'bout her bein' a savage ready to scalp one half of the town and eat the other. Somehow he convinced his brother of such, too, though you'd think a newspaperman would know better. Fella uses his paper to tirade against Injuns more often than not.'

The batwings swung inward again and another man stepped through, pausing to scan the barroom. Tom turned, saw the man glance his way, then at Lucas Hasley. This fella was the complete opposite of the hardcase. An expensive three-piece suit and dove-coloured shirt snugly fitted his large frame. Wire-rimmed oval spectacles framed cold grey eyes. He plucked a derby from his head, revealing thinning brownish hair. His fingernails were cropped short, though his hands evidenced a raw scrubbed appearance. His face, solid and clean-shaven, carried an almost regal expression, though a certain hardness belied that.

Brushing dust from the derby, the fellow threaded his way through the tables and went to Lucas, settling on to a stool beside him.

'That's Clinton, the newspaper owner,' Jeb said before Tom could ask.

'He don't look a whole lot better than his brother, just smarter.'

'Hell, I'm right inclined to agree but he's kept himself clean, 'cept for occasional Injun talk.'

Tom frowned. 'Learned to judge folks in the last twenty years, Jeb. Comes with staying alive. You get so you can look in their eyes and figure whether a fella will draw or come peaceably. If I had to peg Clinton Hasley, I'd say he was the drawin' type. Reckon he's nothin' more than a wolf in sheep's clothing.'

'Well, you best be ready to woolgather, 'cause he's headed this way.'

Tom looked down the bar just as Clinton Hasley oiled a smile across his lips and straightened from the stool. The newspaperman had pegged Tom for something, that much was plain. Tom couldn't imagine what, but he intended to let the fellow play his hand. He got a notion whatever reason he had come to Wolf's Bend for it was about to be given a chance to change direction.

THREE

Clinton Hasley stepped into the Rusty Spur and put on a poker face. Inside, a seething fury made his heart pound and his blood surge. After taking care of a little unfinished business at the paper, he'd spent the last half-hour searching for his no-good dimdot of a brother and this was the last place to look – it should have been the last place he would be. Simpleton or not, Lucas knew damn well after previous brushes with disaster he didn't belong anywhere near a saloon. Whiskey only ignited his ornery side and unreined a temper that was none-too-cinched to begin with. Clinton was tired of cleaning up after him. Sometimes Clinton debated feeding Lucas to the wolves and being done with it, but something told him his brother was a good deal more on the ball than he let on and getting rid of him was a more dangerous proposition than it was worth. Besides, if plans went awry, Lucas might come in goddamn convenient, and, hell, he was kin after all.

He plucked off his derby, gaze narrowing. A spike of anger went through him as he spotted Lucas at the end of the bar.

The fury however was short-lived, replaced with something else – mild consternation and surprise. For on a stool at the opposite end was a man whose reputation had more than once come to his attention. A local hero no one in town had seen hide nor hair of for twenty years.

'Hogan . . .' he whispered. Tarnation, what was a fellow like him doing back in town? It couldn't possibly have any connection to Hargrove, could it? That would be a revolting development, indeed. Another notion struck him: What if Lucas had blundered somewhere and got a manhunter like Hogan on his trail? Clinton had carefully covered his kin's tracks after that last incident with a dove a year back, but maybe Lucas had left a loose end Clinton had no knowledge of. Christ, Hogan was practically a legend in these parts. If Lucas had brought *him* down on their backs . . .

Clinton hustled any hint of vexation and worry from his face. Brushing off his hat, he threaded his way through the tables and lowered himself on to the stool next to his brother.

'You best have a damn good explanation for why you're in here again, Lucas.' Clinton's voice came out a snapping whisper.

His brother eyed him with a vacant look, then grinned. 'Why, Clint, I do believe I got a right to go wherever I please.'

Clinton's cheeks reddened with anger. 'The hell you do! You caused enough trouble in here already. We had a deal, you were s'posed to keep clear of the whiskey and doves.'

Lucas gave Clinton a far-off look. 'Hell, *you* had a deal. I never agreed to nothin'.'

Clinton frowned, knowing it would do little good to argue with him, especially when he had that dimdot look in his eyes. 'You were s'posed to meet me at the paper half an hour ago to figure out what to do about getting close to the Hargrove place.'

Lucas cast him a surly look and suspicion wandered through Clinton: just how simple was that brother of his? Did that arrowhead embedded in his brain make him stupid or just plain meaner? Lucas had always had a hankering to hurt things, animals, people. But after that arrowhead put out some of his lights Clinton began to ponder whether his brother's fondness for inflicting harm hadn't gotten out of control. He suspected certain heinous acts attributable to Lucas, ones involving the recent murders of bargirls. Yet those acts bore the mark of a mind with a higher capacity for misdirection and afterthought than his simpleton brother should have been possessed of.

'I showed up early and you weren't there. Got antsy waitin' on ya and came over here.'

Clinton's eyes narrowed behind his spectacles. He doubted Lucas had spent a moment waiting. 'I had business to attend to and you know it. It couldn't wait.'

'Reckon it couldn't. Might've put a real big turd in your teacup, eh, Clint?'

Clinton struggled to suppress the fury surging through his veins again. 'You best recollect whatever happens affects you, too. It isn't just for me. It's for both of us and I'm damn sick of having to clean up your messes.'

Lucas's eyes darkened, a reflection of fury and viciousness moving across them that made Clinton more positive of the conclusions he was drawing.

'What messes might that be, Clint? Seems you ain't got much right layin' anything at my door, do ya?'

Clinton took a sharp breath. 'What the devil do you mean?'

'You know damn well what I mean. You got your fancy suits and that newspaper, but you ain't no better'n me, Clint. You never were.'

Clinton lost all caution where his brother's hair-trigger temper was concerned. Fury stampeded through his veins like charging longhorns. 'You whore-chasin' simpleton! You're lucky I cover your saddle. You didn't have me watchin' out for your sorry hide you'd be at the end of a rope by now.'

Lucas grunted; the sound had an almost animal quality to it. 'Hell, I just wanted a drink. I ain't causin' no trouble and don't intend to.'

'You never intend to. And this certainly isn't the place you go to not cause trouble. I could have used your help with that little matter tonight, but you were too busy risking our whole operation.'

'Well, hell's bells, we ain't got an operation anyway. That Injun gal ain't goin' no where 'less we just go in and get her out.'

'We already lost two men trying that. She's got something there protecting her, near as I can figure, and I don't know what it is. But I do know we can use it to our advantage, somehow.'

Lucas took a swig of whiskey, wiped a forearm across his lips. 'Reckon we already have.'

Clinton's grey eyes narrowed. 'What the devil's that s'posed to mean?'

A sarcastic laugh escaped Lucas's lips and a vicious glint sparkled in his eyes. 'Reckon I don't have to spell it out for you, Clint. You know well as I do. You didn't need my help tonight.'

'You best not be so loose with your mouth, Lucas. You stand to lose just as much as I do.'

Lucas eyed him and the blank look took over again. Clinton knew the conversation had gone as far as it would go on that point. He decided on another tack, one that might pull Lucas's reins a little tighter. He twisted on his stool, glancing at Tom Hogan, then back to his brother. 'You got any notion who that fella is sitting at the end of the bar?'

Lucas laughed, the expression condescending. 'Hell, I ain't that simple.'

Concern played in Clinton's grey eyes. 'You best hope he hasn't come looking for you, or to put a crimp in our operation.'

'He's got no proof of nothin'. Ain't no reason for him to be interested in us, anyhow.'

Clinton shook his head. 'Manhunters don't always require proof. They just need a stout tree and a sturdy length of rope.'

'You jest recollect I go down you go with me. You're just as guilty by coverin' up that gal's accident a year ago. We'd both get a necktie party, so you'd best deal with him.'

Drawing a long breath, Clinton struggled to control himself. He'd practised at keeping his composure under tense situations endless hours, and along with a knack for forethought and ingenuity it separated him from his brother. 'Hell, let's just calm down and think this through.' Clinton threw another glance at Hogan.

'You always was the smart one, weren't ya, Clint?'

Clinton felt renewed irritation at his brother's sarcasm, but forced it down. 'If he was here to take you in he would have made a move by now, I reckon. Maybe that means we can use him to our advantage.'

'Whatcha mean?' The look of puzzlement in Lucas's eyes was genuine this time.

'If Tom Hogan isn't here for you or to interfere in our plans, we have to make sure that doesn't change. And at the same time we might be able to allay any future

suspicions he's wont to get by setting him off on a
different course.'

'You mean hire him?'

Clinton eyed Lucas, pondering again at his simpleton brother's flicker of perception. 'That's exactly what
I mean. Those murders are downright bad for business
in this town. I think it's my civic-minded duty to do
something about them.'

A startled look jumped into Lucas's eyes. 'That's a
hell of a risk, ain't it?'

'A calculated one, I assure you.'

'I don't like it.'

It was Clinton's turn to be condescending and he
relished it. 'You don't have to. You don't do the thinking
for this operation.'

Lucas's eyes flamed with anger but he held his
temper. 'Think you can convince him?'

Clinton slid off the stool. 'You best hope I can, Lucas.
You don't want him looking too closely at you.'

'We'd be decoratin' the same tree in that case, Clint.
Remember that.'

Clinton flashed Lucas a black look, but his brother
only laughed. He hoped Tom Hogan would be a lot
easier to get through to.

Tom straightened on the stool as Clinton Hasley
stepped up to him, proffering a hand. The automatic
dislike Tom took to the fellow was less intense than the
one he felt for the brother, but it existed nonetheless.
He couldn't pinpoint an immediate reason for it, but he
reckoned the buildings weren't the only thing in Wolf's
Bend with a false front.

'Mr Hogan, I am honoured to have a man such as
yourself in our fine town. Let me be the first to
welcome you.'

Tom gripped the newspaperman's hand and it felt damp and spongy. 'Reckon Lulu Belle beat you to that by about an hour and she has a hell of a lot better bedside manner.'

'Lulu Belle?' Hasley raised an eyebrow. Something about the way he said her name told Tom Hasley damn well knew who she was.

'Ain't important, Mr Hasley.'

The man's grey eyes glinted behind his spectacles. 'Ah, you know who I am?'

Tom nodded, turned back to his drink and took a swig. 'Jeb told me you run the local rag.'

A flash of irritation crossed his face. 'Well, rag is hardly appropriate, Mr Hogan. I run the town's newspaper, that is true. I uphold only the highest of standards in what is presented. Wolf's Bend is growing in leaps and bounds; through my paper, I plan to lead this town into the future.'

Tom cocked an eyebrow. 'Do you?' Sarcasm laced his voice. Whatever Clinton Hasley had in mind for the future, Tom bet the town's welfare wasn't his primary order of business. 'Does that include removing undesirables in the process?'

Hasley flashed the barkeep an annoyed eye and frowned. 'I see Jeb has informed you of my crusade.'

'Might say he's enlightened me enough for me to recognize a fella who gilds his prejudices.'

Hasley reddened and his frame stiffened. 'I hope you do not sympathize with those savages, Mr Hogan.'

'Do I have a choice, Mr Hasley? Some folks would say I'm a savage myself. Reckon you're well aware of that.'

'If you mean killing men for a livin' I am aware of it, but of course it is a noble profession in which you indulge, sir. I am in full support of it.'

Hogan got the distinct impression the man was lying. 'That almost gives me pause.'

'Let me buy you a drink, Mr Hogan. I wish to discuss some business with you.'

Tom kept the surprise off his face. He had wondered what the man wanted and now the cards were laid. He couldn't imagine what a newspaper owner would need with a manhunter.

'Reckon I've had my fill of whiskey for the moment.'

Mild insult crossed Hasley's features and with an index finger he pushed up his spectacles. 'All right, let me come right to the point and propose what I have in mind.'

'I don't come cheap, Mr Hasley. Your paper got enough in the till to pay for me?'

'Price will not be an object.'

'I take the job, it's hundred a day, plus any expenses I care to tack on.'

Hasley's face turned nearly purple and his eyes rounded. 'That's goddamn robbery!'

Tom took a perverted satisfaction in the fellow's discomfort. 'Hell, Mr Hasley, your colours are showin'.'

The newspaperman quickly regained control and cleared his throat. 'All right, I'll agree to your terms, but it comes after the case has been concluded.'

'If'n I chose to accept it at all.'

'I reckon you won't see your way to refusing, sir, not after you hear the facts.'

'That so, Mr Hasley?'

'I assume our illustrious barkeep has told you there have been some . . . well, no fancy way to put this, Mr Hogan, so I'll just say it. There have been some horrible murders. Three women have been killed savagely, along with a respected member of our community and the sheriff.'

Tom nodded, curious despite himself about Hasley's interest in the killings. 'I heard about it. Some kind of animal or something.'

'I reckon it's more than that, Mr Hogan. No animal kills the way this murderer does.'

'Murderer? So you figure it's a person doin' these killin's?'

'I do indeed. And I know who is responsible.'

'Do you, now?' Tom's brow crinkled but he couldn't deny he was intrigued by what Hasley said. 'Why do I get the feeling I hear a snakeoil sale's pitch comin'?'

'I believe that Injun girl, Serene Hargrove, is responsible, yes.'

Tom suppressed the urge to laugh aloud. 'I reckon I see it clearly now, Mr Hasley. Another opportunity to rally for the cause?'

'Hardly, sir. I've seen what Injuns can do to a body, and this smacks of just that. It's well known Comanche mutilate their victims to keep them from chasing them around in the spirit world.'

' 'Cept there ain't no Comanche in this area, Mr Hasley.'

'One Injun's the same as another. Apache or Comanche, it makes no difference.'

'I heard these gals were torn up by some sort of animal. Just how you figure a lone gal can do that?'

'Did Jeb tell you it was her husband who got murdered first?'

'He mentioned it. You figure she killed him then went on to bigger and better things?'

'Yes, that's exactly the way I figure it. She has made a pet of a coyote, in fact. Reckon she's trained it to kill.'

Tom studied him a moment. 'Say what you're tellin' me is true, that she's trained this animal to kill folks. Reckon I might accept she put away with her husband, but what possible interest would she have in killin' bar gals? Or your sheriff, for that matter?'

'It's a well known fact Jothan Hargrove consorted with the sporting crowd, Mr Hogan. She killed him because of it, then decided to finish off the women he'd been with. Pure Injun jealousy. It's that simple.'

'And the sheriff?'

'He went to investigate, of course. Some locals found his body along the trail leading to her ranch.'

Tom threw a glance at Jeb, who shook his head in disgust. 'You spin a fine tale, Mr Hasley. Hard for me to believe a lone gal would be up to such, though.'

'Take a look at my brother, Mr Hogan. He's got a piece of flint lodged in his brain because he chose to take an interest in a woman like that. Facts speak for themselves. Someone is murdering innocent folk in this town and I'll bet you it leads right to her doorstep.'

'Your sense of community overwhelms me, Mr Hasley. Reckon I'll think on what you said and let you know.' Tom didn't have to think it over. He plain doubted Hasley's story was anything more than a load of redskin hate wrapped up in a façade of moral concern. Cowflop pure and simple. He'd seen that sort of thing more times than he cared to count. The West had no shortage of intolerance. He had no intention of taking the case, but it wouldn't hurt to let Hasley stew a spell.

'When should I expect your answer, sir?'

'You'll have it in two days, Mr Hasley. Till then stay out of my way.'

Insult rode Hasley's features again and he appeared about to voice an objection, but it never came.

A scream rang out above the barroom noise. All sound stopped; a hush fell heavy and ominous over the room. Bar girls ceased their coy giggles, 'hands silenced their raucous shouts and gamblers clamped their mouths shut. Startled looks played on their faces. All heads swung towards the sound, which seemed to have come from behind the saloon.

Tom bolted from his stool and headed for the door leading to the back hall. Hasley was in motion an instant behind him, followed by Lucas and Jeb, who grabbed the scatter-gun. A number of the braver patrons and doves took up the back.

Travelling the length of the hall in four strides, Tom reached the back door and threw it open, with a wave signalling the folks behind him to stay back.

He slid his Peacemaker from its holster and edged forward. The hairs on the back of his neck still tingled.

The door led to an alley filled with old crates, barrels and garbage. Their shadowy shapes seemed somehow threatening. Slivers of moonlight sliced across the hard-packed ground.

A bar girl stood a few yards down the alley, outlined by moonlight, quaking hands pressed to her bleached face. Standing over a body lying in the dust, she appeared too shocked to move. Tom's gaze travelled to the still form and his belly plunged.

'Jesus H. Christmas,' he muttered, holstering his Peacemaker. Hasley and Jeb stepped out behind him, flanking his sides. Distantly he heard Jeb utter a gasp of horror.

Tom went to the girl and gripped her shoulders, gently shaking her from her spell. She began shrieking over and over, body rippling with violent quakes, tears streaming from her eyes.

'Ma'am, please try to calm down and tell me what happened.' He kept his voice as even as he could, though the sight of the body was enough to unnerve him more than he cared to admit.

She went quiet, looked at him with tear-filled eyes, lips quivering, head shaking in silent denial. 'I-I . . .'

'Take your time, ma'am. Just tell it straight. Ain't no other way.'

'I-I was comin' in to work, takin' the back way and I found her here like . . . like this . . .' She broke down again and he knew it would do no good to question her further. Wrapping an arm about her shoulder, he guided her to Jeb, who took her inside.

He turned to the body, revulsion rising. 'Christamighty . . .' he whispered.

Behind him two gamblers threw up as they got a look at the corpse. A few others turned tail and ran back into the saloon, unable to handle the sight. Lucas Hasley stood well back against the wall, watching with a glassy-eyed blankness for a moment, then wandered back into the saloon.

Tom scooched while Clinton Hasley stood over him. The newspaperman's expression went stony, strangely dark, and his grey eyes glittered behind the spectacles. He tugged a pad and stub of a pencil from his vest pocket and began jotting notes of some sort. The man wasn't squeamish, that was for certain.

Tom scanned the body. He had seen a lot of death in twenty years, but never anything like this. The woman was barely identifiable, her face shredded nearly clean off. Clean white bone shown through in places. Great patches of her peek-a-boo blouse and skirt had been ripped away. Red hair, matted and tangled, was caked with blood; the sour copper odour made him flinch.

Tom looked up at Hasley, needing to look anywhere but at the body for a moment.

'You know her?' Hasley asked, voice cold.

A stinging guilt rose in his soul. 'Reckon I might. Pretty sure it's Lulu Belle.'

Hasley's brow crinkled. 'Another whore . . .' He tucked his pad and pencil stub back into his vest pocket. 'Another Apache moon, too.' He nodded at the sky, at the bloated face of the moon. In the distance, barely audible, came the howl of a coyote and Tom couldn't suppress a shudder.

'Looks like some sort of animal got her . . .' he mumbled, looking back to the mutilated form, doubting his own words. He'd never known any animal, mountain cat or wolf, to do anything like this.

A chilly wind blew down the alley, and a hushed silence filled the gloom. He studied the area around the body, spotting no signs of animal tracks or a struggle, which puzzled him. He noted other things as well, mentally indexing them, needing to ponder them a bit before forming any conclusions.

He reached out, touched her cold clenched hand, drawing her fingers open. She clutched the double eagle he'd paid her over an hour ago.

'More like an Injun got her, Mr Hogan.' The newspaperman eyed him with an icy indifferent expression Tom didn't care for a lick. Hasley seemed suddenly pious, as if all that mattered to him was driving home his point at the expense of a wasted life.

Under other circumstances Tom might have been inclined to clean his clock, but a strange emptiness rode over him and Clinton Hasley was suddenly the last thing on his mind. Lulu Belle had died horribly and likely alone, after being with him. He wished he had treated her more kindly, not sent her on her way quite so fast, but that couldn't be changed.

'You're a bastard . . .' he muttered, and he wasn't sure whether he was referring to Hasley or himself.

'What's that, Mr Hogan?' Hasley raised an eyebrow.

Tom straightened, bitter blue eyes hard, determined. 'I'll take your case, Mr Hasley, but you won't be payin' me.'

'I'm afraid I don't understand.'

'Didn't reckon you would. Just get the funeral man over here and see to it this woman is buried with the best available.'

Surprise lit Hasley's features. 'You must be joking! The funeral man won't put her in sacred ground and who the hell would bother paying for a whore to be buried that way, anyway?'

Tom gave Hasley a look that stopped the man dead. 'Tell the funeral man it's at Tom Hogan's expense. He's got a problem with that he can talk to me personally.'

Tom brushed past the newspaperman and the few remaining patrons and went back into the barroom. Jeb shot him a glance, but remained silent.

Lowering himself on to the stool, he filled his glass and took the whiskey in a single gulp.

Sometimes there was just too much blood in the West, and sometimes it drowned a man's soul.

FOUR

How much more guilt can you take, Hogan?

He doubted it was a hell of a lot. He had ridden into Wolf's Bend with a saddle-full and now he had more blood on his hands:

Lulu Belle's.

He felt responsible. If onlys had been plaguing his mind since he guided his bay on to the darkened trail leading towards the Hargrove horse ranch. If only he'd treated Lulu Belle better, if only he'd let her stay, if only he'd accompanied her back to the saloon. But none of those mattered because she was dead and he couldn't do a damn thing to change it. He could only vow to find her killer and bring her lost soul a measure of peace.

And relieve your own guilt, Hogan? Isn't that what you're really aimin' for?

Hell, maybe a passel of both.

The spring night had turned colder and his breath steamed out. Ribbons of alabaster and shadow wavered across the hard-packed trail as the full moon glared down through the swaying branches of Quaking Aspen, Engelmann Spruce, and Lodgepole Pine that rose in sheltering canopies to either side of him. Their black shapes creaked with the breeze, and the brush made eerie shushing sounds. The horse's hooves clocked in a monotonous hollow rhythm and the chirping of woodland creatures and sombre calls of hoot owls lent the night world a ghostly aspect.

Try as he might Tom couldn't force the image of Lulu Belle's mutilated body out of his mind. He had likely been the last one to see her alive.

Except for the killer, he corrected himself. He had run across some vicious hardcases in his time, men who held no respect for property or human life and wouldn't hesitate to kill man, woman or child, but he'd never seen a more grisly desecration of a body.

Who could have done such a thing? Or what? An animal? He discounted that theory nearly immediately. To believe a cougar or wolf padded into town, killed the dove then walked off without anyone seeing it seemed foolish. In his study of the death scene Tom had noted not a single animal track. As well, any beast that brazen would most likely be sick with the foam and make a hell of a commotion. He saw no way it could have escaped attention, or specifically killed one woman.

That indicated a human factor at work and in fact his investigation backed that up. For while there were no animal tracks he spotted plenty of others, enough to indicate Lulu Belle had been killed elsewhere and dragged into the alley by someone clever enough to avoid notice.

Other factors substantiated that theory. The blood on the dove's body and in her hair had partially dried, caked in places, and none had pooled on the ground around the body. Given the condition of her corpse, a lack of blood in the dirt seemed impossible, unless she had met doom elsewhere and been transported afterwards.

Where had she gone after leaving him? Some other customer? Tom had questioned the hotel man to see if he had sent her to another room. He claimed she had left and that was the last he'd seen of her; he had no notion as to her destination. Although Jeb expected her back, which lent credence to the assumption she had no other marks, Lulu Belle proved unreliable at times and was wont to wander in when she damn well felt like it.

That left him with little to go on other than Hasley's implications and that wasn't much.

The newspaperman's assertions a half-breed woman named Serene Hargrove had trained a coyote to kill her husband and the local whore population struck him as ludicrous, but a nagging recollection of the man's words about Comanches mutilating bodies to prevent being chased in the afterworld by vengeful spirits stuck with him enough not to discount the theory completely. Could someone have trained a prairie wolf to murder? It would certainly account for the animal not being seen and the body being transported.

Whatever the case, at the moment he had damn few options this was the easiest to eliminate.

Before heading off to the Wolf's Bend *Gazette* office, Hasley had cast a few more accusations in the direction of Serene Hargrove. The newspaperman evidenced little concern over the murdered whore and that made Tom ponder how deep the fellow's hatred of Indians went, and why. He reckoned he could see Lucas carrying a grudge, but the half-wit brother had remained silent the entire time and left a few moments before Clinton. Was Clinton Hasley simply an Injun hater? A nagging suspicion told Tom some deeper motive guided the fellow's supposed acrimony. Perhaps he had some personal reason for blaming the Hargrove woman, or perhaps it was a front for something else. Tom couldn't be sure at this point, but he scribbled the name of Clinton Hasley on his short list of suspects to be investigated.

A howl broke his reverie and he tensed in the saddle. The sound rode eerie and lonesome over the wind, unnerving him. His horse neighed, snorted.

For a moment everything fell silent, then the breeze rustled the leaves. A sudden feeling of being watched came over him and he couldn't shake it. His gaze scanned the trail, searching for signs of anyone lurking in the shadows, but he saw nothing.

A disturbing thought rose in his mind. Whoever or whatever had killed Lulu Belle and the others was still at large and struck on full moons, according to Jeb. Besides doves it had killed a lawman, and even the strongest man could be taken by surprise. He made a mental note to watch his back.

A measure of relief took him as the brush began to thin out, giving way to rolling grass, scattered cottonwoods and evergreens. In the open there were fewer places for a bushwhacker to hide.

In the immediate distance, to his right, moonlight reflected in diamond sparkles from a meandering stream. To the left, miles away, the dark shapes of mountains pierced the night sky. Under normal circumstances the night would have been peaceful, inviting. He'd always preferred the darkness, at least since that day twenty years ago.

You'll never get your soul clean, Hogan. Why bother trying?

The notion took him with a dull shiver and he struggled to force it from his mind, only partially successful. Damn Jeb for getting under his skin earlier; all his talk of facing ghosts, coming back to Wolf's Bend for a reason. While he hadn't given it much thought beforehand – it seemed just a stray thought, to see the old town again, perhaps renew old ties – it had quickly turned into a hell of a lot more than that.

He'd spent twenty years running from the events of that sun-scorched day, gunning down or hanging every hardcase who crossed his path in an effort to stop those ghosts from tormenting him, devouring him. Twenty years of blood and yet he couldn't wipe the memory of that mistake from his mind. Did all that death make anything better, easier to accept? Did it erase the regrets, the guilt, the nightmares? So far it damn sure hadn't. He cursed his sorry hide, wondering just what it would take before he was free, could live with the fact that an inexperienced and mule-headed young man was responsible for losing an innocent life.

Maybe never. And maybe Jeb was right and that's why he was back, to discover if redemption was even possible.

A hundred yards distant he spotted a ranch house bathed in moonlight. Various outbuildings lay in a horseshoe pattern – a corral for training the horses, sheds and a stable. Not a large spread by western standards, but tidy and well kept. He wondered about the man who had built it, Jothan Hargrove. Jeb's knowledge of the man was sketchy. The rancher had ridden into town about two years back and purchased the land outright, setting himself up in record time in the horse raising business. Apparently what Hasley had said about Hargrove was the truth: the fellow, though married to a half-breed Apache woman, rarely brought his wife into town and, in fact, spent far too much time consorting with women of the line. Lulu Belle had been his favourite.

He sent his horse towards the main house, a sprawling rectangular affair of clapboard and neatly trimmed hedges. Gravity pipes leading from a tank fed running water into the kitchen. A steep roof fashioned with hand-split shakes of cypress looked sturdy enough to withstand even the harshest Colorado winters. A wide porch with a wooden awning covered most of the front. Buttery light spilled through a double window, refracting through panes beaded with moisture. Puffs of smoke billowed from the chimney and the air was scented with a woodsy tang.

Another howl broke the night, a low mournful call that made him tense in the saddle. Something sounded . . . *different* about it this time. He wasn't sure what.

Shaking off a quiver of apprehension, he reined up in front of the house, and stepped from the saddle. He tethered the horse to the hitch rail and the bay shuffled his feet and snorted.

The mount was nervous again, sensing some unseen threat. Tom listened, alert for any sound or movement. A low growl came from behind him and he edged around, belly sinking.

Freezing, he peered at the creature that stood in a patch of moonlight beside the porch. The animal squatted on its haunches, peering at him with glassy black eyes that glittered with moonlight. Its coat rippled with the breeze and its ears were pulled back flat against its narrow head. Lips curled from yellowed fangs.

A coyote. Hell, this had to be the animal Hasley told him about. Normally prairie wolves didn't get this close to the house unless they were sick, but he could see no foam frothing from the beast's mouth.

A thought struck him unbidden: this could not be the same coyote he heard howl a moment before. That sound had come from the direction of the trail, and this animal could not have reached the house that quickly.

His hand eased to the handle of his Peacemaker; he slipped the weapon from its holster. Bringing the gun level, he prayed the creature would turn and run off.

'Go on, git!' he snapped, but the coyote didn't move. His finger curled about the trigger. If the coyote attacked he'd have no choice but to fire.

The telltale *shrik* of a shell levering into a rifle chamber behind him sent a chill down his back. He cursed, wondering how the devil anyone could have snuck up so silently.

'If you pull that trigger, stranger, I will pull mine.' A woman's voice. She sounded dead serious and he wasn't about to test whether she was bluffing. He lowered his gun, made no sudden moves.

So much for watching your back, Hogan . . .

'Ma'am, I wasn't intendin' to unless that critter attacked me.'

'Coyote, go!' the woman snapped and the beast whirled and ran off, disappearing around the corner of the house. 'There, now you are no longer threatened.'

'Much obliged, ma'am. If'n you don't mind I'll just turn around so I can see you.'

'Holster your gun before doing so.'

He complied, sliding the piece back into its holster and easing around. Outlined in the moonlight, a vision of Indian beauty, she stood aiming a Winchester at his chest. Stunned, he reckoned he had never seen a more lovely woman, of any race. She wore a two-skinned dress fashioned of black-tailed muledeer, sewn along the shoulders and down the sides, fringed at the side seams and along the hem. A leather belt studded with brass tacks girdled her slim waist and a choker made from hair pipe beads, with spacers of glass, encircled her neck. Braids with hair ties, leather-beaded ornaments in hour glass shapes, fell to either side of her high-cheekboned face. Large dark eyes appeared luminous with captured moonlight and her lips were full and inviting. Her figure was slim but bosomy. Plains type moccasins, fringed at the heel with low cuffs and solid beading in simple geometric design across the insteps adorned petite feet.

Cold reality flashed back in as he peered at the Winchester in her hands. Her finger caressed the trigger and she held the rifle rock steady.

'Wish you'd stop pointin' that thing at me, ma'am. It might go off.'

A crooked half-smile turned her lips. 'Only if you give it reason to. Who are you? What are you doing here? Did Hasley send you?'

Mention of the name took him aback. 'You know Clinton Hasley?'

'He has made me offers for this land. When I refused he sent a man out to "persuade" me.'

'Persuade you? How?'

'He made threats, told me if I did not accept Mr Hasley would use his newspaper and influence to turn the town against an Apache woman, then I would lose everything.'

Tom made a mental note to confront Clinton Hasley about that. Seemed the newspaperman had conveniently forgotten certain information and that spread a new light on his hate for Injuns and this woman. 'You still refused, I take it?'

She gave a sharp nod. 'I did. That man never reached town to bring him the news, however.'

'You killed him?' He raised an eyebrow.

She uttered a small laugh. 'Hardly. But something did. It is not safe to be out here on an Apache moon, have you not heard? Indian spirits might tear you to pieces.'

'That ain't particularly funny, ma'am.'

'It was not intended to be.'

'What are you doin' out here? I thought Indians weren't big on night prowlin'.'

'It must be my white half, then.'

He studied her, puzzled, unable to determine whether she were mocking him or just had an odd sense of humour. When he didn't say anything she let out a small laugh. 'Reckon I don't see anything funny, ma'am.'

'You are ignorant of Apache ways.' She nodded at the sky. 'Do you know why the full moon is called an Apache Moon?'

He felt a prickle of irritation. 'Reckon I'm ignorant of that too, ma'am.'

'You have much to learn, paleface.' She smiled, apparently finding a joke at his expense satisfying, but of course she was the one holding the rifle. 'Apache warriors attack at night only by the light of the full moon because they believe if they are killed in darkness they will wander the afterworld in complete blackness for all eternity.'

'Reckon I picked the wrong night to come here, then.'

'I have no intention of shooting you – unless you give me reason to.'

'You can lower that thing.' He nudged his head at the rifle. 'I ain't here to harm you.'

'Who are you?' She kept the rifle aimed at his chest and her dark eyes studied him intently.

'Name's Tom Hogan. I just came to ask you a few questions.'

'At this hour of night?' Her brow scrunched, as doubt crossed her eyes. 'Questions about what?'

'There was a murder in town earlier tonight. A young woman got torn to pieces.'

'What makes you think I would know anything about that?'

'I'm afraid you can thank Mr Hasley for that. He told me your husband was killed the same way, along with some other gals and the sheriff.'

'I bet that was not all he told you about me.'

He nodded. 'Well, I reckon tolerance ain't his strong suit.'

'He hates all Indians, Mr Hogan.' She lowered the rifle and kept her gaze locked with his. He saw something then, a strange sense of emptiness in her eyes, a lost quality, and he wondered why.

She turned and went up on to the porch, opening the front door. Lantern light spilled across the boards. Turning back to him she said, 'You may come.' He wondered why she had suddenly decided to trust him.

He climbed the stairs and stepped into the parlour, closing the door behind him. Flames leaped in the raised stone fireplace, splashing the walls with dancing light. The room held a small sofa and writing table. A round rug with an Indian weave lay in front of an over-stuffed chair. Baskets with attractive woven patterns in browns and reds rested in corners. Called *tutzas*, they were coiled, of different shapes and sizes, intricately designed. Beside the fireplace rested an Apache fiddle. Its painted sound box, crafted from a hollowed yucca stalk, held one string of sinew attached to a tuning peg. Holes near the top helped to modulate tone. A bow of sinew and wood lay nearby.

She set the Winchester on wall pegs and went to the hearth, lifting a kettle from the fire. Selecting a clay mug from the mantle, she poured steaming brown liquid into the cup and handed it to him.

He took the mug, gazing at its contents and stifling a suspicion she might have decided to poison him instead of shooting. 'You're takin' a chance invitin' me in after what just happened out there, ain't you, ma'am?' He took a sip of the steaming liquid, flinching at its bitter taste. 'What the hell is this?' he asked before he could stop himself.

She let out a small laugh and he reckoned if he wouldn't have been irritated at the fact she kept mocking him the sound might have been endearing. 'An herb tea, Mr Hogan. It gives strength and clarity of mind. You have the wolf in you. He claws to be free. Perhaps the herbs will help you see that.'

His gaze narrowed. 'Don't catch your meanin'.'

She scrutinized him, chocolate eyes probing. 'It is the Apache in me, Mr Hogan, to answer your earlier question. I can tell when a man is no good. I have had plenty of experience in such matters.'

'That so? What does your intuition tell you about Clinton Hasley, then?' He asked it in a more sarcastic tone than he intended and averted his gaze from her dark eyes. She disturbed him, no doubt about that. Her beauty made his innards do funny things and he suddenly felt awkward as a schoolboy at a hug social. But it was more than simple attraction. Because when he looked into those eyes he saw things, some reflection of hidden pain and lonesomeness, a kindred spirit.

'Mr Hasley wants my land. He may get it eventually.'

His gaze went back to hers. 'That's hardly Indian divination. Sounds like you're just restatin' cold hard fact.'

A shadow crossed her features. Her lips drew into a

tight line and for the first time he noticed a small scar near the corner of her mouth. 'Mr Hasley has more in mind than just my land, but I do not know what. He is not someone I would trust.'

'I'm inclined to agree with you on that point.' He threw another gaze around the room. 'If you don't mind my forwardness, how do you support this place? The barkeep told me your husband was killed six months ago. Can't be easy makin' ends meet.'

'I assure you it is not, Mr Hogan. I make dresses and Indian baskets and beadwork for some of the women in town who do not hate Indians. I sell off horses, but that will run out by fall. Then I may have no choice but to . . .' The empty look wandered into her eyes again.

'No choice but to what?'

She ignored him and sat on the low stone edge of the hearth. 'This woman who was killed tonight, was she close to you?'

He shifted feet, looked at the floor, frowned. The urge to say something cutting came over him but when he looked back to her he found himself unable to find the words. Hell, what was the matter with him? What kind of effect did this woman have over him? He suddenly wished he could exchange the tea for whiskey.

He decided to be honest with her, though for some peculiar reason he felt vaguely embarrassed. 'No, she wasn't close. I knew her intimately, though. Reckon she wasn't what most folks would call a lady.'

'You mean a bar woman.' It wasn't a question but he nodded anyway. He felt something akin to shame heat his cheeks. He wondered if she thought less of him for that and wondered even more why he cared.

'Reckon that's as good a description as any. Whatever she was she didn't deserve to die that way.

Neither did the rest of those women or your husband.'

A coldness washed across her chocolate eyes. 'I would not be so sure about my husband, Mr Hogan.' Her voice came hard, condemning, and he wondered why she had made that statement. He wanted to question her about it, but he had not come here to pry into Serene Hargrove's personal affairs. He had come to track down a murderer and whatever else Hasley claimed this woman to be Tom felt sure she was no killer.

'How'd it happen, ma'am, your husband's death, I mean?' He took another sip of the tea.

She crossed her arms, rubbing them, and looked into the fire. 'He went to the stable for some reason I do not know after . . .' Her voice turned brittle and when she gazed back to him the lost look was back in her eyes. Her fingers went to the scar beside her lips and Tom started to put it together. Serene Hargrove's husband was a woman-beater. He was responsible for that scar and now her earlier statement about him deserving death made sense.

'After what, ma'am?'

'It is not important, Mr Hogan. He went to the stable and something killed him. It tore him to pieces.'

'Hasley seems to think you did it, well, with the help of your prairie wolf anyway.'

She laughed, but this time there was little condescension or humour in it. 'I imagine he knows that is not the case.' She said it with such sincerity he wondered if she knew more that she was telling. Had she made more judgments on Clinton Hasley? Her eyes locked with his, again probing, almost challenging. 'Do you believe that, Mr Hogan?'

'Reckon I don't, to be honest. I saw that woman tonight. I saw what whoever killed her did to her body and I reckon you ain't capable of that. Neither is that mutt you got outside.'

'You could be Apache, Mr Hogan.'

'How's that?'

'You are perceptive – is that how they call it? Yes, I believe it is. You know the truth when you see it . . .' Her chocolate eyes glinted. 'Except perhaps within yourself.'

The uncomfortable feeling cinched his innards again and he shifted the subject back to the matter at hand. 'You got any notion who did kill your husband, ma'am?'

She shook her head. In the firelight he saw her black hair had highlights of auburn. 'I do not know, Mr Hogan. Perhaps he made enemies in town.'

'You run this place by yourself, now? Seems a mighty big chore, yet everything appears in perfect order.'

'I do. My husband's nephew used to help, but he disappeared the night Jothan was killed. I have not seen him since.'

Tom raised an eyebrow. 'You reckon he might have had anything to do with the killing?'

'No, Mr Hogan. I am sure he did not. Clay was afraid of my husband and had every right to be. He was a boy, not a murderer.'

'Afraid of him, why?'

'My husband was a cruel man at times. He did not treat Clay very well.'

'What about you? He treat you well?' It came out before he could stop himself and she turned away, gazing into the fire, unanswering.

'Perhaps you should leave, now, Mr Hogan. I find myself growing weary and have much work to do tomorrow. A breeder is coming to inspect one of my horses. I must prepare.'

He nodded, knowing he had overstepped his bounds. He set his mug on a table and went to the door. 'Much obliged for your help, ma'am. If it makes any never-mind to you I'll find whoever killed those women and your husband. And I'll see to it Hasley doesn't have a reason to cast any more blame your way.'

'Remember what I said about the wolf inside, Mr Hogan.' She didn't turn around and after a long moment he let himself out. Going down the porch steps and mounting, he reined around and gigged his horse into a brisk gait towards the trail.

He wasn't sure what he expected to find coming to the ranch, but Serene Hargrove was as far from what he might have anticipated as possible. Her assured manner and upfront approach while vaguely disarming was refreshing, a world apart from the blatant bawdiness and fool's-gold sincerity of the bar doves he was used to.

He drew up just before the trail, plucking the flask from his pocket and downing a gulp. He glanced backwards at the distant ranch house and shook his head. Serene Hargrove had affected him in a way he'd never experienced and that made him damned uncomfortable, yet at the same time eager to see her again. She disturbed something deep inside of him, churned up that aching sense of lonesomeness he always tried to quell with too many whores and too much whiskey.

Tucking the flask into his pocket and heeling his bay into an easy gait, he shifted his thoughts to the only conclusion about the half-breed woman he felt sure of: Serene Hargrove was no killer. She was a victim of circumstance and likely whoever had killed her no-good husband had done her a favour. Any man who saw fit to abuse a woman like that rightly deserved what he got. He couldn't deny the notion of any fella striking her sent a white-hot spike of anger through his veins. The thought of Hasley's false claims came in a close second. With it came a growing sense of protectiveness he wasn't used to. When he confronted Hasley with the facts the newspaperman had conveniently forgotten he would have to temper that, let his manhunter skills take over and not lose his head. He reckoned he'd never had to tell himself that before; since leaving Wolf's Bend he'd been anything but hot-headed, merely a cold calculating thing of vengeance and justice exacted by searing lead, a machine in a way.

You're goin' soft in the head, Hogan. Hell, one meeting with a woman unsettled you that much?

'Jesus H. Christmas,' he muttered, trying to shake off the feeling. He'd spent twenty years seething in his bitterness and he damn well wasn't about to stop now.

Then why are you back?

Maybe the answer to that was a lot more complicated than he thought. Damn Jeb and Serene Hargrove anyway.

Something's out there . . .

The nagging feeling of being watched broke through his reverie and a chill slithered down his spine. It came stronger than before, and the bay stuttered in its step, sensing it, too.

He tightened the reins, steadying the animal. 'What's wrong, boy?' His voice was a ghost. Brow knotting, he scanned the moonlit trail. Every dark shape, every errant shadow seemed suddenly alive and sinister, clutching. A thin mist had come up, spiderweb wisps opaled with moonlight, slinking across the ground. He slowed and the bay began to fight his authority.

Whatever it was gave him more than a feeling of

being watched now. Dread came with it, threat, danger.
Closer . . .

A howl rang out, an eerie shuddering cry that sent a
sizzle of apprehension through his nerves. The sound
wasn't right. No prairie wolf he'd ever encountered
sounded that way.

A sudden thrashing of something large scurrying
through the brush made him jerk his head right. He
glimpsed a vague dark shape, as quickly gone.

'What the hell?' he muttered. The quick movement
and darkness made it impossible to tell what it was,
but it appeared too large to be a coyote or mountain
cat.

A growl came from the darkness, low, throaty, pregnant with threat. His horse gave a sudden lurch,
jerked to a halt, and he was nearly thrown. Only his
tight grip on the reins prevented him from hitting the
hard-pack.

The bay began to dance about and he struggled to
calm the animal, bring it under control. The horse
would have none of it and stamped its hooves, throwing its head back and forth, flouncing from side to side.

Another flash of movement to his right caught the
corner of his eye. A figure, huge and shadowy, lunged
from behind a tree to the concealing shelter of another.

Another howl, ear-splitting and too close for comfort,
sent the bay into spasms of terror.

'What the hell's wrong with you, boy?' he shouted,
straining to bring the animal under control. The bay
neighed in fright and reared up on hind legs. Its hooves
beat the air, slammed down, throwing up chunks of
trail and a cloud of dust. He squeezed his thighs
against the horse's sides but it had no effect.

He cursed the animal, having all he could do to stay
in the saddle. If he couldn't get the bay to calm down

he'd soon be meeting the ground, and it was a hell of a long walk back to town, especially with that thing in the woods stalking him.

'Whoa, boy!' he yelled. The bay responded by rearing again and letting out a terrified neigh. As he fought to get the horse grounded, it slammed down on to the hard-pack. The shock sent a jolt through every bone in his body, almost separated him from the saddle.

With no time to recover, the horse shot straight up. Powerful muscles uncoiling, back arching. Its hind legs kicked violently as it straightened in mid-air. His hands wrenched loose from the reins and his seat lifted from the saddle. His legs yanked free of the stirrups and he sailed backwards.

Suddenly only empty air was beneath him and the darkened trail whirled before his vision. He twisted, endeavouring to get his feet beneath him and hit the ground evenly, only partially successful. He slammed into the dirt on one leg, which swept out from beneath him, sending him hurtling sideways and down. He rolled with the impact, tumbling over and over in a cloud of dust. Gravel bit into his back and arms, tearing his shirt. His hat flew off, and he threw his arms protectively before his face.

Coming to a stop, he wasted no time surveying damage. Whatever caused his horse to throw him was still out there and he had no desire to end up like Lulu Belle. He shot up into a crouch, pain lancing his side and shoulder. His horse bolted, sending clods of dirt flying behind its beating hooves as it raced towards town.

A low growl came from the brush and he tensed. A form moved, snapping a twig beneath its weight. His eyes stung with dust and he caught just a blurred glimpse of a dark shape edging from behind a tree.

Through clouded vision it appeared huge, indistinct, hairy. He couldn't be sure whether it was man or animal, perhaps some sort of bear.

The thing started towards him. His hand slapped with lightning speed for the Peacemaker at his hip. The gun cleared leather in a blur and came level. The dark shape lunged backward in nearly the same instant, obviously aware of the threat, which made Tom doubt it was any animal.

Reflexively, he jerked the trigger. A shot blasted smoke and flame but he had hurried the aim. He missed, heard lead thunk into a tree.

The dark shape hurled backwards into the woods, vanished into the shadows. Sounds of thrashing and snapping twigs retreated deeper into the woodland. He debated going after it, but right now he could barely see, and if it were some sort of animal it had a distinct advantage of knowing the territory and being able to manoeuvre far better in the forest than he.

Drawing a deep breath, he suppressed a shudder. He had come damn close to being another victim of whoever or whatever killed Lulu Belle and the others.

Holstering his Peacemaker, he glanced at the trail ahead and cursed his horse again, for good measure. It was going to be a long walk back to the hotel.

FIVE

The brassy sun glared from a sapphire sky as Tom
Hogan stepped from the hotel and paused to draw a
breath of crisp morning air. Plagued by various aches
and pains from his fall, he rolled his shoulders and
cracked his neck. After walking the distance to town
last night without further incident, he discovered his
horse waiting at the livery.

Sunlight sparkled from water troughs, glinted off
window panes, and coated the street with honey. A
buckboard rattled past and he watched women in frilly
dresses chatting as they bustled along the boardwalks.
'Hands from local ranches meandered into shops for
supplies. Everything appeared peaceful, despite the
murder behind the saloon. Tom Hogan wondered if
anyone gave a thought to Lulu Belle and concluded it
was damned unlikely. Another dead whore made little
nevermind to these folks. But if the killings kept up,
things would change. Fear would spread, begin to
subvert the tranquillity, and folks would get more and
more antsy, tempers more volatile.

It wouldn't take long to turn this town upside down,
especially with men like Clinton Hasley instigating
unrest. Sometimes fear only took a seed and a little

nurturing. The result was always the same, however: vigilantism and someone innocent getting a necktie party. In this case blame would be cast on Serene Hargrove and he couldn't let that happen.

He wondered what Hasley had up his sleeve. The newspaperman certainly had more than the welfare of Wolf's Bend in mind. A man like Hasley was only concerned with his own welfare, and gain.

Starting along the boardwalk, he set the facts together in his mind. Hasley wanted Serene's land. He had made her an offer for it but in itself that meant little, other than Clinton Hasley was a first-class hypocrite.

Second, Hasley had neglected to tell him he sent a man out to the ranch and that man had been killed. That made seven murders counting Lulu Belle's. Tom reckoned he could see where the newspaperman would have kept quiet on that point since he hadn't bothered to mention he tried buying Serene's land, but if he were really so all-fired intent on bringing down a killer and blaming the Indian woman it was a suspicious point to hide.

At the least, Clinton Hasley was a liar. At the most . . . well, that was to be determined. And that's just what Tom had in mind. He didn't like being lied to and he'd damn well let Hasley know it.

He halted, stepping from his thoughts as his gaze lifted towards the Wolf's Bend Bank. A shiver of dread rode him, despite the warming day, and he struggled with the dark memory. A gunshot thundered from the bowels of his mind and he swallowed. A scream echoed from the past. The nightmare threatened to flood his mind, the scene drenched with crimson and gunpowder blue. He could see her face, pleading, terrified—

He shook off the spell and drew the flask from his

pocket, downed a slug. The liquor settled in his belly, calming him. Pocketing the flask, he drifted towards the newspaper office.

He reached the building and stopped, glancing at the painted gild lettering arching across the window that bore the legend Wolf's Bend *Gazette*. Beneath, in smaller straight letters it read, 'Clinton Hasley, Owner and Editor'.

As he opened the door and entered, Hasley looked up from behind a Washington Hand Press. Sleeves rolled up, he was setting type by hand, using wooden characters, locking them into type forms. The air was redolent with the pungent odour of ink. Sheets of paper lay on a long table that ran along the north wall.

Tom removed his hat, which he had recovered from the trail before walking back to town.

'You're up awfully early, Hogan, aren't you?' Hasley's tone said he wasn't particularly happy to see him first thing in the morning.

Tom met the man's gaze. 'Reckon you owe me an explanation, Mr Hasley. I came to collect it.'

Hasley wiped his ink-stained hands on a dirty cloth, a glint of something unreadable in his grey eyes.

'What's on your mind, Hogan? I understood you didn't want my money. Since you aren't working for me I don't know as I owe you much of anything.'

'Reckon I want it even less, now.'

Hasley's brow knotted. 'Don't follow.'

'I took a ride out to the Hargrove woman's place last night. Saw that coyote you blame those murders on.'

Hasley's face darkened slightly. 'I stand by my claim, sir. That woman and her pet are a menace.'

Tom made a disgusted sound. 'Hardly. That coyote is trained to her command, ain't no doubt about that, but it ain't capable of doin' what I saw last night.'

'That what you came to tell me, Hogan?' Bravado overtook the newspaperman's tone and a challenge lit in his eyes.

Tom walked to the long table and slung a leg over the edge, folding his arms. 'Appears you weren't quite truthful with me last night, Mr Hasley. You neglected to mention you made Serene Hargrove an offer on her land.'

Hasley laughed a patronizing laugh. 'And why not? That's a big spread. Too much work for one person and a woman alone certainly can't keep it goin'.'

'And you decided to be her guardian angel and rescue her from her plight?'

Hasley's eyes narrowed. 'Don't care much for your tone, Hogan. Don't care for it much at all.'

'Didn't reckon you would. Let me get right to the point, Hasley. I don't care a lick for bein' lied to. Any man lookin' to hire me best come clean up front or deal with the consequences.'

'Ah, but you said yourself you don't want my money, Mr Hogan.'

'Why'd you really want to hire me, Hasley? To drive that woman off her land so you could take it?'

Anger sparked in Clinton Hasley's eyes and his body went rigid. 'I resent that, Hogan. I made her a legitimate offer right after her husband was killed. At that time I didn't suspect her and figured she'd jump at the chance. After those other killings I began to suspect there was more to it and that's why she wasn't eager to sell.'

'That why you sent another man to persuade her into sellin'? Hear tell he didn't come back in one piece. Any reason you didn't tell me about *him* last night?'

'Didn't think it made any difference.'

'How you figure?'

'One murder or seven, makes no nevermind. It would have just complicated matters and it doesn't change who's to blame.'

Complicated them for himself, Tom reckoned. 'Who was he?'

'Just a fella who did occasional work for me here at the paper. I sent him to make an offer and I believe she killed him because of it. Injuns don't care who they butcher.'

'Why do you want that land, Mr Hasley? You're a newspaperman, not a horse rancher or cattleman.'

'I am merely interested in starting a horse ranch, Mr Hogan. Running the paper has become tedious and I want to move on to other things.'

He was lying; that much was clear by his unctuous manner. 'Find that a mite hard to swallow.'

Hasley's face grew hard. 'I assure you the reason is just what I said it was.'

Tom nodded, not bothering to hide the disbelief on his face. 'What about that brother of yours, Mr Hasley?'

This time he saw a definite hitch in Hasley's expression, as quickly hidden. 'Lucas is a simpleton, what's he got to do with it?'

'Maybe nothin', but I heard he causes trouble now and again. You bein' his kin an' all it makes me wonder if that trouble ain't something you have to clean up.'

'Our conversation is finished, Mr Hogan. I don't like your implications. Get out.'

Tom pushed off the table and set his hat on his head. 'Who says I'm implicating anything, Hasley?' He went to the door, pausing, hand on the handle. 'I recommend you leave Serene Hargrove alone, Mr Hasley. She's a decent woman, regardless of any hate you got for Apaches.'

'That a threat, Mr Hogan? Keep in mind my paper

wields a lot of power in this town and your type ain't always welcome.'

'Don't seem to have caused a problem so far, Mr Hasley.'

The newspaperman cocked on eyebrow. 'No? Well, maybe if I refreshed their memory in a column about some trouble you had here twenty years ago they'd see things different.'

The insinuation was plain and Tom felt his belly twist. Hasley had done his research; he knew what happened twenty years ago and Tom hadn't expected that. He vowed to keep a closer eye on the man. He judged him to be at cross motives, a narrow-minded bigot where Indians were concerned, but most likely it went deeper than that. Hasley's free use of blackmail proved it, as far as Tom was concerned.

Tom's face tightened and his tone went cold. 'Like I said, Mr Hasley, take some friendly advice and leave that woman alone. I reckon she's suffered enough in ways you couldn't imagine. I wouldn't take kindly to her suffering any more.'

Hasley showed no sign of backing down. 'And you take some advice yourself, Hogan. Stay out of my way or I will use every power at my disposal to see to it you are spirited out of Wolf's Bend or hanging from a cottonwood.'

'We understand each other right fine, then, don't we?'

'We most certainly do.'

Tom stepped on to the boardwalk, closing the door behind him. The irritation burrowing under his hide grew stronger. Hasley had gotten the better of him and that didn't happen often. If he had learned anything he solidified the notion the newspaperman was up to no good, but what it was was a mystery. Did he simply want Serene's land and her out of the area to pacify his own hatred of redskins, or was he hiding a more nefarious motive? And how, if at all, did Lucas Hasley enter into the equation? He wondered where the brother was at the moment.

Tom stepped from the boardwalk and headed towards the saloon. He'd gotten nothing out of Hasley, but he still had a second option in mind. Jeb had said he would have to face the ghosts, well, he reckoned he'd make a start with Lulu Belle's. He hoped somehow she could reach beyond her grave to point a finger in the right direction.

'I told you it was a galldamn dangerous thing to do tryin' to throw that manhunter on to that woman's trail!' said Lucas Hasley, as he stepped from the back room of the newspaper office. 'Sometimes you gotta wonder who's the simpler of us, Clint.'

'I can handle him.' Clinton ignored his brother's slight, gaze fixed out the window. He gave himself the edge for that encounter, but he had no delusions where Tom Hogan was concerned. The manhunter was nobody's fool and perhaps he had underestimated him if he had thought he would be so easily taken in. He wondered just how much Tom Hogan suspected. Likely it was plain conjecture with no proof. But if Hogan believed Serene Hargrove and took a notion to work for her, things could get sticky fast and something would have to be done.

Lucas came deeper into the room. 'Hell you can. He believes that woman and his type don't stop till they get what they're after. You should have knowed that, Clint.'

Clinton shot a glance at his brother, who stared at

him with a disconcertingly vacant look. 'What the hell made you an expert on manhunters?'

Lucas gave a lopsided grin. 'Hell, I been outrunnin' 'em long enough, 'long with every other form of lawman you can shake a stick at.'

'You've been outrunning them because I cover your tracks for you. You damn near got caught after killing that saloon gal last year in Dark Creek. Another hour in that town and you'd have been decorating a cotton-wood.'

'Hell, that was an accident and I ain't done it since. Law's got nothin' on me.'

Clinton raised an eyebrow, grey eyes intense, searching. 'You have any more accidents lately, Lucas?'

'What the hell's that supposed to mean?'

'Those women didn't die on their own and you know it.'

'Reckon they didn't, but that don't mean horse spit.' Lucas's gaze drifted from Clinton's. Clinton bet his brother knew more about those killings than he let on. He saw a peculiar darkness in Lucas's eyes, something animalistic and wanton and brutal. It had always been there, ever since he could recollect, but after that Apache flint ended up embedded in his brain Lucas changed for the worse, beating numerous bargirls damn near to death, picking fights every time he walked into a saloon.

At times he wondered why he just didn't leave Lucas to his own devices. Things seemed to have deteriorated since they'd arrived in Wolf's Bend. He had reasoned bringing Lucas to a rowdy mining town would provide camouflage. The town was a den of iniquity and Lucas should have fitted right in. But these killings . . . those were more than he bargained for, but he couldn't prove anything, which either meant his brother wasn't responsible or was playing at being a simpleton a hell of a lot better than Clinton thought.

He studied his brother, searching for any signs that all was not as it was supposed to be, but the blank look was there, as if Lucas was doddering off in his mind somewhere. 'You sure you didn't meet up with Lulu Belle last night?'

'Hell, no! She was s'posed to be meetin' with you.'

'She was s'posed to be meetin' with *us*, Lucas. You never came here. You went to the bar instead. I had the money all set to buy her silence but she never showed up. I figure she ran into something before getting here.'

'And you got a notion that somethin' was me?'

'You have been known to be rough on gals time and again.'

'I ain't the only one, Clint. Don't you forget that. 'Sides, you know damn well I ain't got near the Hargrove place and couldn't have killed that fella or the men you sent out there.'

Hasley eyed his brother, searching for any sign of a lie. 'You're right about that. Something killed Hargrove before he could tell me where the stuff was, and something got our men. Figured after the fella I hired got killed that no-good lawdog could handle it, but it got him, too.'

'I don't see why we don't just bury that gal.'

'You want to risk getting close to the place? Something's killing those folks and I'm not willing to risk my neck finding out what. I can use the paper to get her to leave.'

'That don't mean whatever killed Hargrove will leave with her.'

Clinton Hasley grinned. 'Sometimes you ain't as simple as you appear, Lucas. Whatever's out there seems to be protecting her. Likely when she goes it will, too.'

'Can't we just go in when the moon ain't full and search around?'

'You got a notion it's Apache spirits who only strike on full moon nights? Hell, Lucas, you know that's just what I print in my paper. So far it's just worked out that way, except for that man I hired. Wasn't a full moon when he was killed. That's why I didn't tell Hogan anything about it. I wanted him to think it was that Hargrove woman's Apache ways.'

Lucas's hand went to the scar at his temple. 'Maybe you best not dismiss Injun spirits so lightly, Clint.'

Clinton let out a derisive laugh. 'Reckon we got more to worry about from Mr Hogan than any Injun hoodoo. You best be careful and not show yourself too much so he doesn't get suspicious of you, and for God's sake stay away from any whores.'

An unreadable look crossed Lucas's eyes and Clinton frowned. Lucas had gotten some fool notion into his dimdot mind and that could be bad. He was damned tired of watching every direction, but had no choice, at least for the moment. Until he had what Hargrove left behind, Lucas's luck would hold. He was too convenient a scapegoat to dispose of.

'Surprised to see you startin' the day in a barroom so early, son!' White beard bobbing, Jeb looked up as Tom came through the batwings. Making his way to the bar, Tom slid on to a stool, tossing his Stetson atop the counter. Early morning sunlight streamed though the windows, giving the place a dingy amber atmosphere. The saloon was empty of patrons but a few doves were serving double duty watering down whiskey and wiping out glasses.

'Early bird catches the worm, ain't that what they

say?' He sounded more sarcastic than he intended, but he was annoyed over his meeting with Hasley.

Jeb gave him a suspicious eye. 'What kind of worm you aim on catchin', son? Hear some of them critters taste plumb bitter to bite into.'

'I rode out to Serene Hargrove's place last night. That woman ain't no killer by a long shot.'

Jeb shook his head. 'Never figured she was. That's Hasley's accountin'.'

'Know anythin' about her husband other than he saw some of the doves here? I got the impression he gave her a time of it.'

Jeb shrugged. 'Ornery sonofabitch, far as I could tell. Some of the gals complained about him likin' to inflict pain, treated them rough till a couple threatened to blow his balls to Kingdom Come. After that he kept himself in line.'

Tom frowned. 'Willin' to bet his wife didn't have that luxury.'

'Then I reckon he plumb deserved what he got.'

'What about Lulu Belle, how often she see him?'

'Regular-like. Like I said, she was his favourite, but if you figured her out at all you know she would have given him a third eye socket 'fore lettin' him beat her.'

Tom ran a finger over his upper lip. 'She ever say anything to anyone about him?'

Jeb shrugged. 'Not so far as I know. Why you ask?'

'Serene Hargrove told me Hasley wanted to buy her land. Had to ask myself why would a newspaperman have any interest in a horse ranch.'

'You try askin' him?'

'Yep, but he ain't the most obligin' of sorts when it comes to the truth. But it set me to wonderin'. And the only other one who might know the reason other than Serene and Hasley would be Hargrove himself.'

' 'Cept he's worm food.'

Tom nodded. 'Say he did know, who's the most likely person he would tell, if not his wife?'

Jeb nodded, understanding dawning in his eyes. 'I see what you're aimin' at, son.'

Tom smiled. 'It's a long shot and maybe a lead that goes nowhere, but maybe Lulu Belle can still point a finger towards her killer, least if she knew anything and confided in someone.'

Jeb nudged his head to a dove sprinkling fresh sawdust on the floor. 'You might ask Kate over yonder. She and Lulu Belle were friends of a sort.'

Tom swivelled his head and scrutinized the blonde Jeb had indicated. She was young, no more than nineteen and had hard but attractive features. Too much coral tinted her cheeks and an overapplication of kohl shadowed her eyes.

Tom slid off the stool and made his way through the tables. As he approached, she looked up with expectant eyes. She was younger than he originally thought, the pancake makeup adding a couple years to the impression. She was likely no more than seventeen.

'Hell, cowboy, you're in mighty early for bell ringin', ain't ya? Not that I'm complainin' a-course, 'cause any time with a gent like you's the right time.' She gave him a coy smile and tipped forward, giving him an eyeful of her ample bosoms, which were mounding out of the top of her bodice. This gal had learned her trade early and she spoke with the dubious skill of a practiced calico queen.

He plucked a double eagle from his pocket and held it up. It sparkled in a shaft of sunlight, flashing a golden circle across her face. She cocked her head, an enticing smile oiling her lips, which she moistened with a slow sweep of her tongue.

She reached for the coin but he pulled it away before she could touch it. 'I need a little of your time and some information.'

She giggled with all the sincerity of a snakeoil salesman. 'Hell, for that I'd marry ya, cowboy!'

'Upstairs.' He ducked his chin towards the staircase. He passed her the coin, which she dropped into her skirt pocket. Smile growing wider, she turned and headed up. He followed her down a dingy hallway lit by low-turned wall lanterns.

'Which room?' he asked as she stopped midhall.

'First door to the right, honeybun.' She plucked a key from between her breasts and unlocked the door, shoving it open and giving him a curt giggle.

Stepping inside after her, he shut the door and suddenly she was next to him, running her hands across his chest. He couldn't deny the sensation set bells ringing south of his border but he found himself pulling back, wondering what the hell was wrong with him. She was more attractive than many of the girls of the line he'd been with and under most other circumstances he would have been sorely tempted to give her a turn. But after yesterday and Lulu Belle . . .

Hell, it was more than that and he knew it, because suddenly he saw Serene Hargrove's face in his mind and got all tied-up inside. What the devil was happening to him? He had to be crazy turning down a pretty young thing like Kate. Hell of a time to start comin' down with a case of the morals, he told himself.

'Just need me some information, miss.' He took a step back and she got an insulted turn to her Kewpie doll features. She likely wasn't used to being turned down.

'Hell, cowboy, you ain't a fella's man or somethin', are ya?' Her question came with a goodly measure of spite and maybe even an edge of hope. He suddenly felt sorry for the girl, who seemed reaching out for some sort of perverted approval he couldn't give.

'Hardly. Jeb told me you were friends with Lulu Belle.'

The girl shuddered, any look of insult vanishing from her face, replaced by genuine regret and fear. 'She was my best friend. Terrible shame what happened to her, ain't it?' Her voice sounded small and suddenly brittle, as if all fronts had come down, if only for a moment.

He nodded. 'I want you to tell me about her.'

'Reckon a gal don't tell secrets out of school, cowboy.' Her voice had lost its momentary innocence and the practised edge was back.

Frowning, he plucked another eagle from his pocket and held it up. 'School days are over, I reckon.'

She snatched the gold piece from his hand. 'Reckon I was always a quick learner anyways. What you want to know?'

He went to the window, looked down into the alley below, a shudder working through him at the memory of the bargirl's bloody form lying in the dust. 'What was her connection with Jothan Hargrove?'

Turning, he gazed at her, seeing her expression darken. 'He hired her most of the time. She was his favourite.'

Tom nodded. That much he knew. 'She ever mention him saying anything interestin'?'

She smiled, catching his meaning. 'She told me he had some big scheme in mind that would make him richer than Jesus B. Christamighty, 'cept he wouldn't tell her what it was, least that's what she told me. Said if she was real good and did what he wanted he'd cut her in on it.'

'What did he want her to do?'

'Somethin' about settin' him up with a fella who could do a job for him, but she wouldn't tell me what it was, only that it involved someone important and she planned to take advantage of that and Hargrove at the same time. Lulu Belle was an enterprisin' sort.'

'No idea what the job was?'

'Sorry, sugar. If I knew I'd tell ya.'

He doubted it, but likely that was all the information she would disclose. He wondered what the hell Hargrove had been up to and who he wanted to be put in contact with. Could it have been Clinton Hasley? What reason would Hargrove have need of a newspaperman for?

On a whim, he asked, 'What do you know about the Hasleys? Ever been with either of 'em.'

A look of fear crossed her face and he knew he had his answer. 'I been with both of them, and you best stay away from them gents. Especially that simple one.'

'Why's that?'

'He gets gawddamn rough on his gals, like that Hargrove fella, only worse. He ain't right in the head, neither. Plumb out of his saddle, if you ask me.'

'What about those other murdered girls and Lulu Belle, they ever been with Lucas?'

She let out a scoffing laugh. 'Hell, cowboy, all of 'em have. Lulu Belle used to arrange it for him, 'specially after he got into fights in the saloon and couldn't come in for a spell.'

'What about Clinton?'

'Him, he was more discreet 'bout it, but some of the gals came back with a few extra lumps in places that weren't feminine, if you catch my meanin'.'

Disgust crossed his face. 'I catch it. Lucas likes to beat on his woman, treat 'em rough, and Clinton likes to keep things quiet. Reckon he would, runnin' the *Gazette*. Might not look good for a respected member of the community to be consortin' with doves.'

'You got it, sugar. You sure you don't want an early bird special?' She batted her eyelashes and let a hand drift sensuously across her fleshly front.

'Maybe some other time.' He dismissed the dove and stood in the room for long moments, considering what she said. Hargrove engaged Lulu Belle to set him up with someone who could benefit him in some unknown enterprise. The murdered dove also sent girls to both Hasleys. He had new pieces to his puzzle, but did they fit together or lead in separate directions? For the moment he set them aside until he had more information. Trouble was, it left him unsure of his next move. He had hoped Lulu Belle might point him in a direction, and maybe she had, but which one?

Shaking his head, he left the room, went down the hallway and descended the stairs. Nodding at Jeb and grabbing his hat from the counter, he headed out through the batwings.

The sun had risen higher and the day was quickly warming. He paused, pondering his next move, but any decision was stopped cold. A shout drew his attention to a spot a hundred yards down the boardwalk, in front of the mercantile. Gaze following the disturbance, his face pinched at the sight of a man standing atop an over-turned crate.

Hell.

He no longer had to wonder where Lucas Hasley had gotten off to. The hardcase was gesturing forcefully from atop his perch to a handful of spectators listening with eagerness on their faces. Tom couldn't make out what the fellow was saying, but wagered it had something to do with Injuns in general or Serene

Hargrove in particular. A sinking feeling taking his belly, he let out an under-the-breath curse and started forward.

'She's a threat to all decent folk!' Lucas's sharp yell punctuated the murmuring of the folks standing before him. He stabbed an arm in he direction of the trail leading out of town. 'She's a gawddamn Injun and you all know they ain't a lick of good! They ain't nothin' but savages, every last one of 'em! An Injun did this to me!' He jammed a beefy finger to the upraised scar at his temple. 'An Injun put an arrowhead in my brain so I couldn't think straight no more. That's what those savages do to innocent folks, I'm here to tell ya. An' they don't stop there, oh, no, that ain't the half of it. They cut up your loved ones and steal your children and feed 'em to the wolves!'

The subtle murmuring turned up a notch and Tom didn't like the way the townsfolk were responding to Lucas's diatribe. Likely nervous already about the killings, it wouldn't take much to work them into a frenzy.

Tom halted, just behind the hardcase, arms folded. A glimpse at Lucas Hasley's eyes gave him a moment of pause. He saw no blank look of a simpleton there now, merely a calculated fever, a sly purpose that told him the man had more on the ball than he'd figured.

'I'm tellin' ya, Serene Hargrove is an Injun devil!' Lucas's arm gestured with force, palm outward as his hand swept in a dynamic arc. 'She's the one who done these killin's and she won't stop till we burn her out and string her up from the closest—'

'That's enough, Hasley!' Tom snapped, anger surging through his veins.

Lucas stopped in mid sentence, head swivelling, brow furrowing. Hate and viciousness flashed in his small eyes. 'Go away, manhunter.' The hardcase's voice lowered, pregnant with threat.

Tom refused to be intimidated. 'What the hell you up to, Hasley?' His gaze locked with the hardcase's.

'Gettin' rid of a killer, Hogan. A no-good, Injun squaw killer of whores. Get the hell outta here while I do my law-abidin' duty.'

'Your type don't know the meanin' of the word. Get off that box 'fore I take you off.'

Hasley's eyes exploded with unadulterated fury. The man was dangerous as a cornered badger, instant to anger; that fact was plain. No telling what he was capable of.

He found out. Without a second thought Hasley launched himself from the box and Tom, caught by surprise, had no time to prepare.

The hardcase carried over two-hundred pounds of solid muscle and all of it crashed into Tom with the force of a bull slamming into a barn door. The impact knocked an explosive burst of air from his lungs and sent him reeling backward and down. He slammed into the boardwalk, a plume of dust billowing.

Hasley, atop him, drove a blocky fist straight towards Tom's face.

Tom jerked his head sideways, avoiding most of the force, but it caught him a glancing blow that sent hot-iron streaks of pain through his jaw. The hardcase's fist continued past, slamming into the boardwalk, cracking a plank. He let out a roar and Tom gathered his senses enough to take advantage of Hasley's momentary concern over his hand.

Tom hoisted his feet upward and locked them around Hasley's bull neck. Jerking backwards in nearly the same motion, he threw the hardcase off him. Lucas crashed onto the planks and rolled sideways.

Tom pushed himself to his feet, unsteady, knowing he had only a moment before the hardcase recovered. He launched a side kick as Hasley got to his knees. His bootheel clacked Hasley flush in the jaw and propelled him over and back.

That should have been it. The kick was hard enough to take down a mule, but Lucas sprang to his feet, lurching forward.

Tom, caught wallowing in his astonishment, tried to sidestep but for a large man Hasley's speed was deceptive. The hardcase arced a chopping blow that sent Tom staggering backward into to the mercantile wall.

A cascading roar filled his brain. The blow had stunned him, made his legs rubbery. Ringing pain vibrated through his face and teeth.

Murder in his eyes, Hasley stepped in, threw another punch that would have put Tom's head through the shiplap siding. Tom snapped a forearm up, deflecting the blow just in time.

Countering, Tom buried his right deep in Hasley's gizzard. The hardcase gasped and stutter-stepped backward. Tom seized the advantage, swinging a vicious uppercut from the ground.

Hasley somehow recovered his senses enough to jerk his head out of the way and the uppercut caught him a glancing blow, doing little damage.

The miss threw Tom off balance. The hardcase countered with a stiff left cross that slammed into Tom's cheek; he felt like he'd been clocked with an anvil. His senses dipped south and darkness threatened to swallow his mind.

Hasley swiped a hand towards him in a wild arc, the man's long jagged nails raking across Tom's face, opening gory streaks. Blood trickled down his face and he let out a sharp curse.

Hasley wasted no time surveying his work. He hurled Tom backward, pressing him to the wall, jamming a forearm against his Adam's apple and exerting pressure nearly enough to crush his windpipe. Tom gasped, vision blurring and a cottony sensation moving in from the edges of his brain. He was suffocating and in another moment the fight would be over, possibly along with his life.

He grabbed Hasley's forearm, struggling to force it away. It felt thick as a fence post and didn't budge.

As blackness crowded the corners of his mind, he summoned all his strength in a desperate last measure and jerked his knee up, depositing it directly where it would do the most damage. Hasley's eyes rolled up and he let out a strangled sound.

The hardcase's forearm dropped away and Tom swung a hard looping punch that came without much power, but contacted with a satisfying *clack* that dropped Hasley to the boardwalk. The hardcase crawled about on hands and knees, then heaved a gout of vomit on to the dusty broads. He fell back against the wall, fluid and blood dribbling down his chin. Eyes blank, he struggled to get back up.

'It's over, Lucas,' a voice cut in and Tom looked behind him to see Clinton Hasley stepping on to the boardwalk. He went to his brother, kneeling. 'What the devil are you doing?'

Lucas made gagging sounds, unable to answer.

Clinton turned to look at Tom. 'Mr Hogan, I sincerely hope you have better things to do in the future than beat up simpletons.'

Tom eyed him, in no mood for clever retorts or parrying. 'Hell, your simpleton was incitin' a riot against the Hargrove woman, Hasley. He's a mite smarter than I gave him credit for or else you put him up to it.'

Hasley's face took on a look of insult. 'I assure you I had no knowledge of this. Had I known, I would have stopped it. I prefer more subtle methods of getting a job done.'

He turned and shoved an arm beneath his brother's, hauling the hardcase to his feet then guiding him down the boardwalk. The handful of townsfolk dispersed, leaving Tom staring after the pair and wondering if he were strong enough to even walk back to his hotel.

SIX

The predawn air was crisp and the bloated orange moon was dipping behind the mountains in the west. The first streaks of grey painted the horizon and birds twittered happy songs. Somewhere a whip-o-will sang its lonesome call.

Tom Hogan considered how deceptively peaceful it all looked, as he guided his bay along the trail leading towards the Hargrove ranch. The woodland seemed alive and waking, with no hint of the danger that lurked within its nighttime shadows.

The nightmare had come again.

It was always the same, a hellish dust-coated world where he relived the day he rode from Wolf's Bend in a tangle of guilt and self-blame, rode as fast and as far as his horse would carry him, never looking back.

You killed that woman. . .

That's what the haunting vision told him, taunted him with over and over until he considered putting a bullet through his brains to escape the torture. He hadn't pulled the trigger that day, but he might as well have. He was responsible, any way he looked at it, and held spent twenty years running and smiting every no-good hardcase he tracked down to make up for it.

Things are changing, Hogan. You aren't the same . . .

Wasn't he? Something felt different inside him and he wasn't sure whether it started with returning to Wolf's Bend or Lulu Belle's murder.

Or with something else.

Someone else.

Serene Hargrove.

Even before the nightmare he slept little. Pain humming in every corner of his body from his encounter with Lucas Hasley, he had collapsed on to the bed, staring up at the fly-specked ceiling. Before long, his thoughts had turned to the half-breed woman, but not in a capacity relative to the case. Instead he'd spent the time dwelling on the sensuous turn of her lips, the loveliness of her mocha-cream skin, chocolate pools of her eyes, and the enticing curves of her body. He also wondered how she'd feel locked in his arms and why she pushed all thoughts of young bar doves out of his mind.

It buffaloed him and was something he wasn't used to. Tom Hogan had spent twenty years keeping himself free of all attachments, confining any time spent with women to whores and passing relationships that meant nothing more than a few hours of companionship, a fleeting measure of time where he didn't have to live with the god-awful emptiness inside his soul. It pained him to admit he treated those women with little thought or respect, even with words of cruelness or spite, at times, as he had Lulu Belle. He reckoned that kept them at the proper distance, kept them from making him confront the fact that he carried something more inside than a driving compulsion to dispense justice and repent for the sins of an impertinent youth too damn cockeyed about being a hero to use a lick of good sense.

Serene Hargrove was different, dangerous to a man looking to ride the wind and never face a life where something else mattered other than bitterness and self-reproach.

Then why are you here? he asked himself, shaking his head. Why had he saddled his horse before the sun rose and set it along this trail towards her ranch? He knew better. He had become an expert at avoiding such entanglements and hardening himself against the fickle ways of the heart.

He drew up, sighing, good sense warning him he should turn back and resume his investigation of Clinton and Lucas Hasley and the murders in Wolf's Bend instead of proceeding to Serene's ranch. He'd told himself that countless times since waking from the nightmare and on the way to the livery, to saddle his horse, to no avail.

Because here he was, for reasons he couldn't fathom, needing just to see her, talk to her, even if only for a few moments.

Heeling his bay into motion again, he forced his thoughts back to the case.

He had concluded Lucas Hasley was more than just a simpleton with an arrowhead jiggering his mental processes. The hardcase wanted to further a vendetta against Indians, just as his brother did. But while Clinton Hasley might use his paper and fancy words to turn the town against Serene Hargrove, Lucas was more inclined to act on his hate, imperil her. Kate said the hardcase beat doves; that fact, put together with the scratches Tom had across his cheek and the fellow's brutish strength, put him at the top of the list for murder suspects. Yet something nagged Tom about that theory. On the face of it it appeared too simple, too obvious. Something was missing, some key element. A motive, at least for some of the killings. What reason would Lucas have to kill Jothan Hargrove? Perhaps that had something to do with Clinton's offer for the dead man's land. But what about the sheriff or his brother's own messenger? Even if Clinton wanted Serene's land for some concealed plan, Lucas had no reason to murder at least two of the suspects.

Tom's mind drifted back to his first night in town. Lucas Hasley had come into the bar shortly after Tom. Could he have gone after Lulu Belle? But why kill the dove if she arranged gals for him and his brother, or was a go-between for Jothan Hargrove?

If Lucas were the murderer, why hadn't he gone after Serene yet? Why was he inciting the townsfolk against her instead? Was Clinton keeping a rein on him somehow?

A sound caught his attention, pulling him from his woolgathering. To his surprise, he discovered he had ridden farther along the trail than he realized. The woodland had fanned out and patches of reddish gold were streaking the eastern sky. Sparkles of amber reflected from the stream a hundred yards to his right. He surveyed the area, searching for whatever had made the sound, and, squinting, he made out two shapes by the stream. He realized then what the sound was, a low chant embraced by the breeze.

He guided his horse in that direction. As he drew closer he saw the shapes were those of the young woman and the mangy prairie wolf she had befriended. They sat on an Indian blanket, an ornate woven basket nearby. Legs tucked beneath her, she looked up at the sound of hoof-falls.

As he approached, the coyote stiffened, rose to all fours, ears pinning to its skull, the hair on its back standing up in a bristly wave. A low growl issued from curled back lips.

The young woman stopped chanting and whispered, 'Coyote . . .' The animal sat on its haunches, remained quiet, but kept a wary eye on Tom as he reined up.

'Ma'am.' He touched a finger to his hat. 'Ain't it a mite dangerous for you to be out like this with all the killin's goin' on?'

She looked up at him, chocolate eyes shimmering and soft. 'I am in no danger, Mr Hogan.'

'Why would that be, Mrs Hargrove?' he asked before he could stop his manhunter instincts from taking over.

She gave a soft laugh. 'Because Apache spirits protect me, and I have coyote.'

He stepped from the saddle and tethered the horse to a tree branch. 'Reckon I wouldn't be so confident about that, ma'am. I caught a glimpse of the killer the other night on my way back to town and I ain't so sure Apache spirits or your mutt would be much of a match for it. I was lucky I had my gun.'

She glanced at the Peacemaker on his hip. 'You have killed many, but you are not a cruel man, Mr Hogan.'

A twinge of unease twisted in his belly. 'I do what I have to do, at any rate. Why are you up so early?' He glanced at the blanket and basket. 'Hell of an hour for a picnic, ain't it?'

She smiled a thin smile, and he knew she saw right through his brusque manner. 'I do not sleep well at night, Mr Hogan. I come here for peace, to listen to the morning creatures and chant songs of healing and hope. Before, it was dangerous for me to sleep at this time and I have been unable to break the habit.'

He folded his arms, brow bunching. 'Dangerous? How's that, ma'am? Seems like bein' out here with a killer runnin' loose would be worse.'

A pained expression crossed her dark eyes. She stood and turned towards the stream, wrapping her arms about herself.

'My husband, as I said, was a cruel man. He would fall into a drunken sleep. At first I thought I was safe when that happened and would sleep, as well. But he would awaken and. . .' Her voice broke and for the first time he saw another side of her, a hurt she kept deep inside.

'I think I can see where it's goin', ma'am. You don't have to say it.' His voice came low, comforting, and that was an awkward change for him. He couldn't recollect the last time he'd given anyone solace, himself included.

'No, Mr Hogan I do not mind.' She turned to him. 'I can see I am safe with you, though I see other things in you as well that are . . . *disturbing*. My husband would awaken and demand things from me, things a wife is required to do for her man. He traded the headman twenty horses for me and considered me his property, to do with as he pleased.'

A burst of anger went through him. 'He had no right to demand that, ma'am. Something like that is either given or it ain't. Anything else is a hangin' offence in my book.'

'I never realized anything different, Mr Hogan. My Apache village was different, but in many ways the same. My white mother found that out when my Indian father took her in a raid. After a time, she accepted Indian ways. I think it just wore her down to a point where she could no longer tell right from wrong and I grew to be that way as well.'

His disgust mixed with compassion and his voice softened. 'It's plain wrong and it doesn't have to be that way, ma'am. Can't say I think any better of your band either, if they'd swap a woman for horseflesh.'

Her dark eyes locked with his and he saw pain within her, fear, as if she had decided to let him glimpse it, to understand the tortures she had endured. Her husband had treated her in ways she didn't deserve and somehow she had accepted that, lived under that constant domination. It puzzled him. Offence had always been clear cut to him. It someone stepped over that line he retaliated in kind or in the case of criminals killed them. For her, it was different, partially because of her upbringing with an Indian band, but mostly because of a pattern pounded into her by a cruel cold-hearted excuse for a man.

'It is no longer that way, Mr Hogan.' She brushed a tear from her eye.

'Reckon I'm worried it might be if Hasley has his way.'

'Mr Hasley will have this ranch eventually. I am enjoying its peace, now, but I know I will run out of horses in a few months, and making dresses and baskets does not bring enough money to keep it running. I may make it until autumn or possibly the end of the year, but after that. . .'

'After that, what? You said something about having no choice the other night.'

'I believe I would go back.'

He couldn't hide his shock. 'To your band? Hell, they traded you for horseflesh and you want to go back? That don't make sense.'

'I am Jicarilla Apache, one of the *Diné*, The People. My real name is Singing Wolf. It is where I belong. It is their way.'

His brow bunched and he frowned. 'Hell of a way, then.'

A gleam appeared in her dark eyes. 'Perhaps, then, I need a man who will not trade me . . .'

Unease made him take a step back and he averted his gaze. Something fluttered in his belly. It confirmed what he thought: Serene Hargrove was a dangerous woman for a man too long alone. 'You ain't somethin' to be traded, ma'am. You're free to choose and there must be some way to keep things goin' so you don't have to sell out to Hasley or return to your band.'

'I can see no way, Mr Hogan, but perhaps something will present itself.'

'Hell, if you're in such an all-fired hurry to go back why don't you?' It came out harsh and he immediately felt sorry for it, but the thought of her returning to such a life disturbed him more than he cared to admit.

'If I return I am promised to another.'

'An Apache?'

'Yes. His name is Striking Wolf. We were betrothed. My husband took me from him. Striking Wolf was angry, wanted to kill Jothan but the headman forbade him to be near me.'

'You ain't got anything for this Striking Wolf, I take it?' He couldn't tell why he felt relieved at that notion.

'I did not love him and never would, though I believe he cared deeply for me. He is a hard but proud warrior. He vowed he would await my return. If I go back I will have no choice but to be his.'

He turned back to her and her chocolate eyes were probing. It would be so easy to become lost in those dark pools, and he cursed himself for his growing attachment. Coming back to Wolf's Bend had been a mistake; coming here had been a bigger one.

'I make you uncomfortable, Mr Hogan . . .' A slight smile turned her full lips, inviting lips that brought out desires in him he'd never felt with bar doves.

'You might say that. I ain't used to being read so well.'

'I cannot read everything, Mr Hogan.' She paused, eyes searching. 'You asked me why I was out here so early. I would ask you the same question.'

He looked towards the stream, refusing to let her see into him at that moment. 'I don't sleep so well at night either sometimes, Mrs Hargrove.'

She stepped closer and touched his shoulder and he damn near started. 'Why do you not sleep well, Mr Hogan? I would like to know.'

He took a deep breath, gathering his courage. He'd never told anyone of the nightmares, merely borne them alone in the depths of the Western nights. He hadn't realized till now just how dreadfully lonely that was, how much he needed to tell someone, tell her. 'I have . . . nightmares sometimes, things that haunt me that ain't conducive to a restful night's sleep. Reckon I spend lots of time just starin' at hotel ceilin's or up at the stars. Sometimes it's easier to sleep during the day or just drink them away.'

She recoiled and, glancing at her, he noticed a pained look on her face. He wondered what he had said to make her feel that way.

She gazed at the ground, looked back up. 'My husband was worse when he drank. He would use a whip, then.'

'Jesus H. Christmas!' he blurted, burning with hate for a man he didn't know.

'Only the scars remain, now, Mr Hogan. It is all right. I live with them and they will always be there to remind me of what happened. In a way that is good.'

He struggled to keep his voice calm. 'Don't see how that's possible.'

A thin smile softened her face. 'When I look at the scars I realize my life is no longer that way and I am lucky. Whatever happens with this ranch and in the future I am better now. I will not be whipped again. You must learn about your scars the same way.'

'No one ever whipped me, ma'am.'

'They do not need to. You do it yourself.'

A prickle of irritation took him. 'Don't see how you can say that. I make my own choices and wouldn't do that to myself.'

'No? These nightmares that haunt you, they are the scars, Mr Hogan. And you add more lashes with each passing day.'

He turned away, his innards twisting. 'I can't accept that, ma'am.'

'Tell me of these nightmares, then . . .'

'I never told anyone, don't know why I should, now.' Bitterness poisoned his voice and he felt the need to push her away.

'Because as long as you don't you will accept it, as I did with my husband. You will take the beatings, though you struggle to defy them, and they will simply hurt you more.'

'Your husband died, ma'am. My demon ain't got that option.'

'In some ways, Mr Hogan, I was lucky he did. It is a cruel thing to say, but I am glad he is gone. I do not know if I would have been strong enough to come to the realizations I have with him alive, but that is for the Spirit Above to know and not me. Your nightmares will not die, you are right. But you will have to make a choice to view the scars and live, or simply exist until the nightmares beat you to death, till the wolf inside devours you.'

'I have no wolf, Mrs Hargrove.' His belly cinched and he fought against what she was saying, but damned if he didn't see a certain logic in it. The scars, the wolf inside. Jeb's ghosts. It all started and ended with him, didn't it?

'Why do you do what you do, Mr Hogan?'

'Manhuntin', you mean?'

She nodded.

He shrugged. 'Tryin' to make things right, I reckon. Protect folks from men the likes of this killer here.'

'You are lying, Mr Hogan. Please tell me the reason.'

Her bluntness took him aback and irritation burrowed under his skin. But she was right, he had been trying to avoid telling her, barely even aware of that fact.

He drew a deep breath, face forming into tight lines. 'I do what I do because my debt is too large to ever pay off.'

'Your debt, Mr Hogan? What could you possibly owe that would require so much bloodshed?'

A flash of anger glinted in his eyes he really didn't intend for her. 'What's the value of an innocent life, Mrs Hargrove? How much worthless blood has to be spilled to make up for a single decent person losing theirs because a boy didn't know a goddamn lick about bein' a hero?'

Her voice softened, almost a whisper. 'Tell me of the nightmare, Mr Hogan. Please . . .'

Emotions roiling inside him, he spun away and suddenly the nightmare was there, layers of time peeled back. The scenery around him vanished. A blistering summer day in Wolf's Bend replaced the tranquil woodland and gurgling stream, a panorama of crimson and dust.

Heat waves rose in rippling waves and dust clogged a young man's nostrils as he stepped from the saloon and headed down the boardwalk, a spring in his stride. Tom Hogan felt the gold of the West jaunting through his veins and slid his Peacemaker in and out of its tooled leather holster. He had practised long and hard, entire days sometimes, shooting at cans down by the stream and he was fast as greased hell and ready to take on the territory. He had just told Jeb he wanted to be a manhunter, wanted to chase down hardcases and Jeb had accused him of being a starry-eyed eighteen-year-old who needed to settle in his britches a bit before he got himself killed. He knew Jeb was merely concerned, but, hell, he had honed his skills to a razor edge and all he needed now was experience.

His gaze lifted to the peaceful dusty street, which baked under a mid-August sun. Wolf's Bend wasn't the place for him any more. Nothing happened here. There hadn't been so much as a pie stealin' in nearly a year. How was a fella s'posed to be hero under those conditions?

He spat and with gusto kicked a stone across the planks. A whole wild west existed out there, ripe for picking, and Tom Hogan was going to carve out a reputation as a master gunfighter who brought down the worst types of hardcases and made the territory safe. By damn and diddle he was!

Thunder shattered the tranquil shell of the street and he jolted, despite himself.

A shot. His gaze jerked towards the direction from which it came – the bank. Jesus H. Christmas! The bank was being robbed.

He spotted the sheriff popping out of his office, hitching his rig around his waist. Tom ducked his chin at the bank and the sheriff gestured at him to stay back.

Hell, no! He wasn't about to miss out on this. It would be his first case; here was a chance to gain a passel of that experience he needed.

He took a step off the boardwalk and halted, a

twinge of trepidation twisting in his belly and he suddenly wondered if shooting a human being would be different from shooting a can. No matter. A hardcase wasn't quite human anyway.

Was he?

He jogged along the street and the sheriff waved him back more violently, but Tom refused to accept the lawdog's direction.

The bank window shattered in an explosion of glass, great glittering shards spiraling to the dusty board-walk as a bullet ploughed through.

The sheriff stopped in his tracks, a starburst of crimson splashing across his chest.

Tom froze, eyes wide and heart racing. The lawman crumpled to the ground and fell face first into the dust.

He had never seen a man killed and it shocked him. He suppressed an urge to retch. He froze in place, mouth hanging open. 'Christamighty,' he muttered.

The bank doors burst open and a man wearing a bandanna over his lower face stumbled out. Arm locked about a woman's throat, he dragged her along in front of him as a shield. Sun glinted off the blue metal of a Smith & Wesson clutched in his free hand. Terror had turned the woman's face into a tearful mask; her mouth moved in a silent plea for help.

The hardcase waved the Smith & Wesson in a threatening arc. Townsfolk scurried for cover inside buildings. 'Send that money on out here!' he shouted towards the open bank doors and a terror-stricken teller shoved a large canvas bag out on to the board-walk.

'Pick it up!' he ordered the girl, jamming the gun to her temple. He leaned sideways, arm still wedged against her throat, so she could grasp the bag. Straightening, the robber dragged the girl a few paces along the boardwalk, heading for a sorrel tethered to the rail.

Tom started forward, forcing his fear down.

The hardcase spotted him; fury flashed into his eyes, which narrowed to a squint. Then he laughed, as Tom's hand hovered over the handle of his Peacemaker.

'Get the hell back to yer mammy, boy! Ain't no place for a young'un.'

'Let her go, you sonfoabitch!' he yelled, the loudness of his voice unable to disguise a tremble in his words that failed to command respect.

The man bellowed another laugh. 'You got a notion to try and stop me, boy? Don't make me kill you. I just want to ride on out of here. I'll leave this here filly on the trail after I'm far enough away. Maybe she'll even be alive.'

The woman mumbled, 'No . . .' and tears streamed down her face.

Tom calculated the odds of shooting around her and killing the robber before he could pull the Smith & Wesson's trigger, but it would take precision aim, and that would take time, more time than the hardcase would give him.

'Let her go, mister.' A moment of indecision gripped him and he wondered what an experienced manhunter would do in this case. Unsure, his hand eased the Peacemaker from its holster.

The hardcase's eyes grew more serious. Tom's breathing went shallow and sweat streamed down his face. He knew the robber was ciphering whether he could keep the woman in front of him until he reached his horse, likely deciding that was the easy part. Then would come a moment where he would be open when he hoisted her into the saddle and climbed in behind her. After, the hardcase would have to rein around and ride off, exposing his back as a target. That's when Tom would bring him down.

Tom raised his Peacemaker with deliberate slowness, showing he wasn't about to back down. He fought to make his voice steady, authoritative. 'You can't make it, mister. Let her go and throw down your gun.' He had failed. The words quivered. His nerve buckled.

The Peacemaker started to jitter as his hand quaked. He fought to control it, unsuccessful.

The hardcase saw it and a sudden thought flashed plain in his eyes: one threat existed and Tom was it. The man had a clear shot at him and shifted the gun from the girl's temple towards the boy who stood open in the street.

On instinct, he lunged sideways. Throwing himself to the ground, he rolled, coming up behind a barrel.

The hardcase adjusted his aim and fired a split second later. Lead sizzled by Tom's cheek.

The girl started shrieking.

'Shut the hell up or I'll blow your brains out, lady!' the robber yelled, fury in his voice.

She apparently didn't hear him above the sound of her screams and kept on shrieking. Terror taking over, she struggled in his grip, kicking at his shins and fighting to get free.

Jim saw it coming then and a crushing sense of powerlessness settled over him. The hardcase jerked the Smith & Wesson back to her temple, exposing a section of his right side in the process.

Tom had one chance to stop the tragedy and jerked the Peacemaker's trigger.

Two gunshots thundered simultaneously in his ears, in his soul, blending into one haunting echo. With sinking horror, he knew he had blown it, hurried his shot because of inexperience and fear.

His bullet missed.

The robber's did not.

'*Nooo!*' Tom screamed, the sound drawn out and reverberating into memory.

The woman's brains exploded out the opposite side of her head in a gory spray of blood and bone and the hardcase flung her body sideways. Swinging his gun around instantly, he fired a second shot at Tom. Lead punched into the barrel and water spouted to the ground.

With a cry of rage, Tom jerked the Peacemaker's trigger five times, emptying the chamber.

Blue smoke clouded his vision and its acrid scent singed his nostrils.

Starbursts of blood stitched a line down the robber's shirt and he danced backward, arms flopping crazily, legs buckling in two different directions.

He toppled over a rail and slammed to the ground in a plume of dust, twitched, then lay still.

Tom straightened, staring, frozen for dragging minutes. Townspeople, emboldened now that the threat had passed, flooded into the street. Murmurs rose to excited voices, filling the air. Some cried over the woman who had been murdered, while others shouted congratulations at him for stopping the robbery.

'Hell, son, you're a hero!' a cowhand yelled, slapping him on the back as he passed.

For an eternal moment he stared at his smoking Peacemaker, then turned and ran into an alley and vomited into the dust. Tears ran down his face as he retched, and after he finished he collapsed against the wall and sobbed until the sun began to sink and the numbness left his body, but not his soul.

A hand gently touched his shoulder and he jerked from his memory.

Through blurry vision he looked to see Serene staring at him, compassion on her face, sympathy in her eyes.

'I rode out that night . . .' His voice was almost a whisper. 'Never looked back.'

'You did not kill that woman, Mr Hogan. That man did, and he paid for it.'

'I killed her just as sure as he did. I should have just let him ride off with her. If I had she would still be alive. But I wanted to start a career, be some kind of goddamn hero.'

'You do not know whether that man would have left her alive.'

He pulled away, drawing a long breath. 'Don't you think I have tried to tell myself that a hundred times over? It don't matter because she's dead and I had no business doin' what I did. If the sheriff hadn't been trying to tell me to get the hell out of the street he might have lived, too. He might have saved her. I got innocent blood on my hands, Mrs Hargrove. It ain't ever goin' to come off.'

'So you continue killing that man over and over?'

He turned to her, emotion clutching in his throat. He had never quite seen it that way, but she was right. He did kill that fella again and again, and again and again he saw that woman's face in his nightmares, saw her brains spattering across the boardwalk and heard her shrieks echoing through his mind.

'If that's what it takes.'

'It will not help, Mr Hogan. No matter how many men you kill. Your scars will always be there, as will mine. That woman is dead and you have avenged her as well as anyone ever could. Now you must learn to look at your scars and know you cannot change what has been. Let them show you your true strength instead of your weakness. As I have done. If I had not my husband would be forever influencing my course. I will not let that happen any longer. You should not, either.'

'I don't know how . . .' he whispered. Twenty years was an eternity of blame, of guilt. How could he let that go now? It was all he had lived for and with for such a very long time.

'Release the wolf, Mr Hogan. Free him.'

He glanced out at the stream, lost in the scarlet mists of the past, struggling to throw off the after-effect of the nightmare. He felt empty inside, drained. Perhaps telling her what happened had helped in some way, started some sort of healing process he wouldn't have imagined existed.

As he turned, Serene Hargrove stepped forward and instinctively he took her into his arms, holding her as the sun splashed the countryside with gold and warmed the day.

At last he pulled away, going to his horse and mounting. He looked down at her and she made two fists, crossing her arms over her chest in the Indian sign for affection. 'Remember the wolf, Mr Hogan . . .'

He nodded, words locked in his throat. Reining around, he rode off, telling himself he was a damn fool for leaving, but some things couldn't be hurried and this was one of them.

Half-way down the trail he drew up, taking a deep breath and pressing his eyes shut, opening them. He reached into his pocket and pulled out the flask, gazing at it for long moments then hurling it into the woods.

Gigging his horse into an easy gait, he rode towards town.

SEVEN

The tide had changed in Wolf's Bend.

As Tom rode into town, head full of thoughts of Serene Hargrove and the way she had felt in his arms, he slowed his bay to a walk. He had spent hours half in a daze, thinking over what she said, about scars and wolves and going on with life. Now, for the first time in twenty years, he knew he had a choice: to go on living a life of bitterness and blame or to accept what had happened and realize he had done all he could to repent for the sins of the past.

But before he could make that choice he needed to deal with the problem at hand. He would see to it Serene kept her land and was not forced to return to Striking Wolf and a life she no longer accepted nor wanted. She was used to the freedom of running her ranch and he wasn't about to let Clinton Hasley take it away from her.

An atmosphere of gloom pervaded the dusty streets, contrasting with the bright sunlit day. Though he saw the usual number of folks hustling along the boardwalk their manner appeared strained, vaguely apprehensive. He heard hushed barbed-tones, caught snippets of conversations relating to the murders and the 'half-breed living just outside of town'.

Perhaps he hadn't stopped Lucas in time yesterday and the hardcase's little speech had fertilized the seed of fear growing amongst the townsfolk. He shook his head, vexed at the notion Lucas's diatribe could have taken hold so fast. He wondered if there were more to it, some unknown factor.

Downstreet he spotted a cluster of men and reckoned that meant no good. Seven of them, ranchhands judging from their clothing and rugged appearance, each face a mask of agitation, eyes darting, mouths cinched into tight lines. Tom had witnessed the same look on the faces of vigilantes and posses coddling a bloodlust. It wouldn't take much to galvanize these folks into regretful action.

A cry disturbed his thoughts and he reined up. A boy dashed along the boardwalk, a bundle of Wolf's Bend *Gazettes* tucked beneath his arm. The lad waved a copy with his free hand and shouted: 'Evenin' edition! Read about the murders in Wolf's Bend! Extry!'

A sinking realization told him what had pushed the town closer to the edge, and that Lucas Hasley wasn't the only party responsible.

As the boy ran in his direction, Tom dismounted and tethered his horse to the rail.

'Paper, mister?' the boy asked, a hopeful look on his round features. Tom nodded, plucking a silver dollar from his pocket and handing it to the lad. The boy's eyes widened.

'Rest is for you, son.' He took one of the papers and scanned a headline in bold, large point type: 'Is Apache Woman Coyote Murderess?' The article, penned by Clinton Hasley, spent numerous paragraphs linking the recent murders with Indian black magic in general and Serene Hargrove in particular. He never came right out and blamed her, but the implications were clear – and worse than outright accusation. He pointed a finger in her direction with subtle and sometimes blatant conjecture, encouraging folks to form their own conclusions.

'Christamighty!' he said between clenched teeth. He crumpled the paper, clenching it in a white-knuckled fist. He shot a glance at the newspaper office down the street and started towards it. The newspaperman would answer for this or Tom was going to see to it another Hasley brother was on the receiving end of his fist.

You're losin' your cool, Hogan. That ain't the way to handle it . . .

He ignored his manhunter voice of reason. Words hadn't worked with Hasley before and it was time for action. The newspaperman's article had placed Serene's life in danger and he would answer for it.

Tom threw open the door and a startled Hasley looked up from behind the press. The fellow's face froze upon seeing the look in Tom's eyes and Tom slammed the door.

'What's the meaning of this invasion, Mr Hogan?' He put on an air of bravado, but a nervous light danced in his grey eyes.

Tom's tone went icy. 'I told you to leave Serene Hargrove be, Hasley.' He took steps deeper into the room. Clinton Hasley straightened and backed up and Tom suddenly wondered if the man had a gun concealed somewhere and would attempt to use it.

'She's a murdering savage as far as I am concerned, Hogan. I print what's right, not what a man such as yourself tells me to. It's my civic duty.'

'You printin' this cowflop just makes this town more

antsy. They're like to do somethin' foolish and that woman ain't guilty of anything.'

'The hell she ain't!' Hasley's face reddened. The man wasn't one to be intimidated easily. 'She's killed four women and three men and I aim to see to it she is run out of this town or hanged, guilty of murder.'

Rage overwhelmed Tom then. He threw the paper aside and lunged at the newspaperman, grabbing two handfuls of the fellow's shirt, and swinging him around. Hoisting Hasley up against the wall, he pressed his face close, fury in his eyes.

'You listen to me, Hasley. You best print a retraction 'fore you're the one hanging from a tree. You wouldn't be the first fella I killed.'

'Don't threaten me, Hogan. I ain't a man who'll abide by such.' Anger laced in Hasley's tone, defiance.

'You'll abide by whatever I tell you, and I'm tellin' you anything happens to that girl and you'll wish that killer was the one who got hold of you instead of me.'

The newspaperman did something unexpected then. Tom realized rage had overpowered good sense and he was caught off guard. He expected Clinton Hasley to be all brains and little brawn, but he was wrong.

Hasley suddenly knifed both arms between Tom's, snapping them outward, breaking the manhunter's grip.

The newspaper owner followed with an arcing punch that struck Tom a glancing blow and rattled his senses. Tom took a stuttering step backward. Shaking the cobwebs from his head, he overcame his surprise at the man's resistance just in time to block a roundhouse right thrown with enough force to take his head off.

The move threw Hasley off-balance and Tom launched a punch that caught the newspaperman squarely in the jaw. Bone met bone with the sound of two bricks colliding. Hasley took the blow with merely a glitch in his step and kept coming.

A flashing thought made Tom wonder what the hell the Hasley stock was made out of. Though he didn't look it, Clinton was as strong as Lucas.

Clinton looped a punch from the floor. Tom jerked his head out of the way and countered with a chopping left to the temple that staggered Hasley. He followed up instantly, a vicious uppercut that should have put Hasley's lights out.

The man somehow got an arm in front of his chin, deflecting the blow enough to send it sailing past his face and throw Tom off balance.

Hasley seized the advantage and buried a fist in Tom's breadbasket. Tom gasped, air exploding from his lungs.

Hasley stepped back to measure his next blow, and Tom forced himself to spring up, launching an unexpected right at the same time. The punch ricocheted off Hasley's temple.

The newspaperman blinked, staggered backward, eyes rolling up. Legs buckling, he crashed into the printing press, remaining upright only by default. He wasn't out, merely stunned momentarily.

Tom moved in for the kill, cocking an arm.

The blow never came. Something crashed into the back of his head and the last thing he saw was the floor rushing up to meet him.

'Gawddamn lucky for you I came 'round when I did,' said Lucas Hasley, setting a wrench on the table. 'I saved your sorry hide.'

Clinton Hasley wiped blood from his lips and eyed the form of Tom Hogan sprawled on the floor. 'You best wipe that gloat off your face, Lucas. He beat the hell

out of you yesterday, too. You're fortunate that isn't all
with that little stunt you pulled.'

'He got lucky. 'Sides, looks like your little stunt's the
one that got him riled.' He nudged his head towards
the crumpled paper lying on the floor. 'What'll we do
with him, now?'

'Throw him in the jail till tonight. It's empty since
that no-good sheriff got his. Maybe when the moon
comes up we'll leave him for that coyote killer.'

Lucas grinned. 'You wouldn't know who that was,
would you, Clint?'

Hasley cocked an eyebrow and glared at Lucas. The
man was an idiot but he had a certain slyness that all
the Apache arrowheads in the West couldn't drill out of
his brain.

Clinton's eyes narrowed. 'I got my suspicions . . .'

Lucas laughed and looked out through the window,
eyes going blank for a moment. 'Those folks out there
are gettin' awful antsy. Reckon after I toss this fella in
jail I might help that along a little.'

Clinton considered objecting, thought better of it.
With Hogan out of the way perhaps his brother's little
tirade against Injuns yesterday could be turned to
their advantage. The article had thrown wood in the
fire and soon the townsfolk would be ready to act. But
he had to be careful, because one miscalculation and
the plan would fail. He decided it would take only
another article or two to work the town into a fever
pitch. If things were pushed too soon they would lose
their nerve. Vigilantism had to be nurtured and hanging a woman was an iffy prospect without laying the
proper foundation.

'Give me a couple more articles to get them in the
proper state. Don't make any moves till then.'

'I don't see why I have to wait—'

His eyes darkened. He was damn sick of his brother, questioning his authority. 'Because I told you to! You best not forget who's running this operation.'

Lucas's eyes met Clinton's and for an instant Clinton got the impression Lucas would challenge him and readied himself.

After tense moments, Lucas's eyes got a far-off look and he frowned. 'Reckon you know best . . .'

Clinton couldn't tell whether his brother's tone held mockery but something told him Lucas had backed down too easy. 'Drag him out the back way and don't get seen. Take his gunbelt off, too. We don't want him gettin' out.'

Lucas nodded, bent and shoved both arms beneath Hogan, hoisting him up and dragging him towards the back.

'And Lucas . . .'

He glanced up at Clinton. 'Yeah?'

'Make sure when the time comes you don't go with any mob. I don't want you associated with any more trouble, even if it works to our advantage.'

'Hell, I hate them Injuns. I wanted me a chance—'

Hasley's face twisted into an angry mask and Lucas stopped. 'You heard what I said. You best not do different, 'less you want that killer after you . . .'

Their eyes met and Clinton knew imbecile or not Lucas understood the threat perfectly.

Tom Hogan awoke with a mule stomping on his skull. At least that's what it felt like to him. Pain thundered across the back of his head and nausea twisted in his belly. He opened his eyes, stared up at a blurry sky of slate grey. Confused, he lay still, waiting for his vision to clear and his senses to fully return. The last thing he recollected was fighting with Hasley in the newspaper office, then the lights had gone out and now he was here, wherever here was.

As the gauze swept from his vision, the sky became a pitted ceiling. He discovered he was lying on a cot and he tried to sit up. A mistake. The room whirled and the nausea pressed into his throat. His head pounded with a vengeance. Struggling to keep his stomach down, he swung his feet to the floor and put his face in his hands, taking shallow breaths. He pressed his eyes shut, waiting for the spinning to stop, opened them and glanced about.

He was in a jail cell and he reckoned from the cidery light streaming through the grimy window across the room roughly two hours had passed since he'd been in the newspaperman's office. His fingers probed the back of his head and he felt a huge goose egg and dried blood. Someone had hit him from behind and he was damn lucky it hadn't cracked his skull. He ventured a guess: Lucas. The hardcase must have been in the back the whole time.

Through sheer willpower, he forced himself to his feet, fighting the spins for a moment, then steadying himself. He staggered to the bars, gripping them and jerking with all his strength. They wouldn't budge and he hadn't expected them to.

He cursed, peering around the room. His gunbelt lay on the desk on the opposite side; he had no way of getting to it. He searched for anything long enough to reach it, saw nothing. The office held a desk, a small table and little else.

You're stuck in here, Hogan. This is what going off hot-headed gets you. Now what do you do?

Sounds reached his ears from the outside and he paused, listening. A muffled aggregation of angry voices, rising and falling, punctuated with shouts and cheers. Someone was inciting them into action and he wagered it was Lucas Hasley. The hardcase was seizing the advantage and there was nothing Tom could do to stop him.

Defeated, he let out a long breath and slumped against the bars. He had no way out of this cell and if those voices told him anything they said those men would be riding after Serene within moments. She might fend off one or two with the help of that animal, but she would stand no chance against a handful.

A sudden crash jerked him from his thoughts. He looked up just as the front door flew open. A figure stood silhouetted by waning sunlight. Tom squinted, trying to make out who it was. The man came in, easing the door shut behind him.

'You Tom Hogan?' the man asked, stepping deeper into the room.

Tom nodded. 'Who're you?'

The man stepped close to the bars and Tom saw he was young, more a boy than a man, with sandy blond hair and a scared rabbit look in his blue eyes.

'Name's Clay Hargrove.'

Surprise took Tom's face. 'Jothan Hargrove's nephew?'

The young man nodded. 'You know who I am?'

'Serene told me you disappeared the night your uncle got killed.'

Clay Hargrove bowed his head, eyes fixed on the floor. 'I ran, Mr Hogan. I ain't proud of the fact, but I can't deny it, either. I heard sounds that night, horrible sounds, in the stable, like some animal was just tearin' the hell outta him. I heard his screams too and I reckon I got plumb frightened. Never was the brave sort, anyhow, not with Jothan around.'

'Why you back after six months?'

The boy looked up, lifted his gaze to meet Tom's. Tom saw raw honesty there, a genuine reflection of guilt that he had seen too many times in himself. 'I spent a lot of time thinkin' 'bout how my uncle used to beat Serene, Mr Hogan. I spent an equal amount feeling like hell 'cause I never lifted a finger to stop it. I let it happen and it tore me up inside, but I was too goddamn a-feared of him to do any different.'

'So you came back lookin' for forgiveness?'

'No, not really. I just came back to make sure she was all right. I reckoned after they found Jothan dead the town might blame her for it, and I got to feeling guilty about that. I knew she wasn't nowhere near that stable when he was killed, not after the way Jothan whipped her that night. I figured she might need my help. I grew up a lot in six months, Mr Hogan.'

Tom studied the younger man, seeing sincerity in his eyes, but his voice came hard. 'Six months is a long time. She might have been hung by now.'

Clay Hargrove shifted feet, averted his gaze. 'I didn't think about that, but you're right. I was a coward, Mr Hogan, and I can't change that.'

Tom nodded, respecting the young man for admitting it. 'She's all right for the moment and that's what matters.'

'But she won't be soon and that's why I came here. To stop what might happen. When I rode in yesterday, I was just in time to see the fight you had with that Hasley fella. I heard what he was sayin' about Serene and knew it was a load of cowflop. But I know how these towns get lathered up and that kind of talk could be right dangerous. I wasn't sure who you were, only that you seemed against him, so I kept my eyes open. Earlier, I saw you go into Clinton Hasley's paper with a hellfire look on your face after seein' that article he printed. Didn't see you come out for a spell and it got me to wonderin' if somethin' happened. I hid out back, then caught sight of Lucas draggin' you here. I waited a spell to make sure he didn't come back, and broke in.'

Muffled thunder came from outside, the rumble of hoofbeats, an indeterminate number of them as they tore through the street. Clay went to the door and peered out, dust clouding into the office as he did so.

'What's happening?' Anxiety turned to ants in Tom's nerves.

'Riders, seven of 'em headin' out of town. Reckon Lucas got them stirred up enough. He was down there carryin' on 'bout Injuns 'fore I came in.'

'He with them?'

Clay shook his head. 'Not that I can see.'

'You have to get me out of here.'

The boy turned, nodding. 'How? Ain't no key around.'

'Hand me my gunbelt.' Tom ducked his chin towards the desk. He gathered up his hat, which lay on the floor by the cot, and set it on his head.

Clay went to the desk and scooped up the rig, bringing it to Tom, who strapped it around his waist. 'Get back.' Clay complied, going across the room.

Tom drew the Peacemaker and triggered a shot at the cell door lock. The blast sounded like cannon fire in the confines of the room and made his head throb with renewed violence. The door popped open. Holstering the Peacemaker, he ran across the room and outside. His horse stood tethered beside another animal, which he guessed belonged to Clay Hargrove.

'Fetched your horse from the livery after Hasley scooted it away. For some reason, it wandered back there.'

'It's got a habit of doin' that,' Tom said with a note of sarcasm. Gripping the horn, he swung into the saddle. 'Hell, you comin'?'

Clay peered at him, fright jumping into his eyes.

'I done my penance, I figure, Mr Hogan. You're on your own past here.'

Tom studied the boy, seeing fear get the better of him and he figured it was little use arguing the point. He could use the help against seven men, but Clay Hargrove would be no aid if forced.

'Obliged for the break-out, at any rate.' Tom reined around. Clay stood still, looking at the ground.

Tom gigged his horse into a ground-eating gallop. Dust clouds rose behind him and dirt spewed from the bay's hooves. He had damn little time; Serene couldn't hold off that many men for long.

In the parlour, Serene Hargrove stared out at the waning day, arms wrapped tightly around herself, wondering if she would still live in this house when the year ended. Would she lose the ranch to Clinton Hasley because she could no longer afford to stay here on her own? In a short while the horses would all be gone. The few women in town who bought dresses and baskets from her might keep her going for another month or two, but even then she would not be able to hire anyone to repair fences or patch roofs. As well, she had heard the talk the other Hasley brother spread in Wolf's Bend after her husband died. He hated Indians and few in town showed sympathy for a half-breed Apache. Perhaps at first none believed his accusations she killed her husband, but it was only a matter of time until they did.

A sigh escaped her lips and her face darkened with despair. Her heart felt heavy, her Apache soul laden with sorrow. Had she unburdened herself of Jothan's cruel domination only to return to her band and be placed under the control of another? She was no longer a part of the Apache world, though she had told Tom Hogan different. Perhaps Striking Wolf loved her in his way, but he would never allow her the freedom she had now and she did not wish to spend the days of her life as a squaw woman.

Tom Hogan had told her she had a choice, but she did not see it. Because if that were true she would choose to stay on this land with him, and she doubted that was possible.

A tear slid down her cheek. His face rose in her mind, and she could see his bitter blue eyes, the strong lines of his face. Tom Hogan was a man tortured by the wolf of his past. He blamed himself wrongly; he let the wolf inside devour his compassion, his vulnerability, as she had let Jothan devour hers.

But, no, that was not exactly right. Because those qualities were still there, as hers had been. The wolf only guarded them, perhaps. Beneath his brusque exterior, buried under layers of bitterness and blame she saw a noble caring man. A man she could love in a way she had never loved her husband or would ever love Striking Wolf.

Tom Hogan did not yet know it but his wolf was free. It had escaped the moment he told her of his haunted soul. Perhaps he would understand in time.

A choice? If the Spirit Above granted it, she would choose to love Tom Hogan, and have him love her in return.

She made her decision. No matter what happened with this ranch she would not return to her band. Never. If Jothan's beatings had taught her anything, they had taught her strength, the ability to see life was not to be lived under the dominion of another.

Tom Hogan, she knew with everything that made her one of the *Diné*, would not prey on her vulnerability or try to chain her. He would not treat her cruelly. But would he want to be with her, a woman the town would brand a pariah, a murderess? She could not force him, but said an Apache prayer he would want to release himself to her the way she wanted to release herself to him.

Dusk was approaching. The parlour bloated with sepia shadows and gloom settled over the land.

A sound reached her ears, and with it dread gripped her soul.

Her gaze focused on the far end of the land and her heart skipped, then pounded in her throat.

In the encroaching dusk she saw them, riders approaching at a gallop. The muffled beating of hooves crescendoed like gathering thunder. They carried rifles and intent showed plainly on their hardened faces, even from this distance.

She froze, skipping back in time, and for an instant the riders vanished and it was Jothan riding in, drunk, his face twisted with anger and hate. The blacksnake snapped in her memory and she flinched reflexively, the sound a scar on her soul. A gasp escaped her lips and she fought to control herself, focus on the riders. Jothan was dead six months. He would never hurt her again. She would not cower inside and accept punishment, not from her memories, not from anyone. She would not let them take her dignity, even if they took her life.

Serene whirled and ran to the wall, grabbing the Winchester. Levering a shell into the chamber, she drew a deep breath and said a prayer to the Gans, the mountain spirits, for strength and victory. Going to the door, she gathered her courage and stepped outside to defend what was hers and claim the remnants of her pride.

EIGHT

The forest opened into rolling land and Tom Hogan felt a measure of hope rise within him, but the feeling was short-lived. Although the riders weren't that far ahead and he had pushed his horse to the limit, a lot could happen in the space of moments when a vigilante band got the scent of blood.

Breath clutching, he spotted the riders spread out in a V formation around the front of the house. Serene stood on the porch, a rifle jammed to her shoulder, levelled on one of the men while the others skipped left and right, darting closer, then back, yelling, taunting her.

A surge of raw anger shot through his veins. He swore he'd kill the first one who touched her.

Calm down, Hogan. That's the sort of thinkin' that got you in trouble with Hasley. Use your goddamn head!

'Yah! he shouted, arrowing forward, cutting the distance in half in seconds.

The riders whooped, curses punctuating the air. Serene kept the rifle levelled on one of the men, her face dark, determined.

'Which one of us you gonna shoot, Injun woman?' one of the men jeered and she shifted the rifle to him.

'You will be first,' she said, voice steady.

126

The man guffawed. 'Judas Priest, the little Injun's gonna shoot me first, boys! Whatta you think of that?'

The others bellowed laughs and two climbed from their horses, scurrying to get around to her side. She shifted the rifle to one then the other and they halted, some of the devilment going out of their faces. They weren't particularly worried, but neither wanted to take the chance she was serious enough to pull the trigger.

Tom reached them then and the man who was doing the talking spun around in his saddle.

'Who the hell are you?' he demanded, face growing dark, obviously aware Tom posed a much bigger threat than a lone woman with a rifle.

'Get out of here, mister, 'fore you regret it,' Tom said.

The man spat, wiped the back of his hand across his lips. 'What right you got comin' here and tellin' me to leave, fella? You best take a look how many of us there are.'

The two on the ground remained still, but another on horseback snapped a lucifer to life, preparing to light a torch. They intended to burn the ranch house.

His hand slapped in a blur of motion to his Peacemaker; it seemed suddenly to appear level on the man with the torch.

'Drop it or take a third eyehole.' His voice came icy and the man knew he meant it.

The torch holder got a look of fright in his eyes and let the torch slide from his hand. It hit the ground, the match following, sizzling out.

Something stopped Tom for an instant, a movement at the corner of his eye. Whatever it was scurried around the stable, a large shadowy shape. Then it was gone. It might never have been there and he had more pressing matters to focus on. He shifted his attention to the spokesman.

'Reckon I gave you your ridin' papers.'

Barely controlled anger rode the man's face. He was itching to start something but some shred of good sense prevented it. 'This here woman's responsible for murdering them folks in town, mister. We aim to see to it she pays for her crimes.'

Tom shifted his aim, levelling on the man. 'This woman is guilty of nothin' but trying to live her life in peace.'

'Hell she is! She's got a goddamn wolf doin' her dirty work for her.'

Tom shook his head. 'No coyote killed those folks. I caught a glimpse of what did and it wasn't no animal or woman, take my word on it.'

The spokesman seemed to consider what Tom was saying. For all their furor they were basically decent folk, frightened and riled by Hasley, solid citizens caught in a fever. None of them wanted to die and likely none wanted to kill a woman, either.

'You say you seen it?' Doubt held sway in the man's tone.

Tom nodded. 'It damn near attacked me the other night. I took a shot at it but missed. Only a matter of time till I get it.'

'Who the hell are you anyway?'

'Name's Tom Hogan.'

'The bounty hunter? Christ . . .' Fear leaped into the man's eyes, along with a healthy measure of respect. 'There's seven of us. We could get you, you know . . .' Confidence had drained from his voice. He plainly didn't believe it, nor did he want to risk a move.

Tom's face went hard. 'But I'll kill you first, mister. Don't make a move you won't live to regret.'

The spokesman appeared to think it over, glancing at Serene, then to his men, back to Hogan. 'Reckon we might have made a mistake, Hogan. This woman don't look like the killer, if what you say is true.'

'You got my word on it, fella. You want your killer you start lookin' in the direction of Lucas Hasley.'

'Hasley . . .' the man muttered, obviously putting two and two together. While Tom had no proof Hasley was responsible for killing anyone, he didn't mind throwing a little grief the hardcase's way.

The spokesman reined around. 'Come on, fellas, reckon our work here is done.' He spurred his horse into a gallop and the others followed suit. Tom watched them go, vanishing down the trail. He slipped his Peacemaker back into its holster.

Serene lowered her rifle and met his gaze.

'Get in the house, Serene, and bolt the door.'

'Where are you going, Tom Hogan?'

'I got some unfinished business with Lucas and Clinton Hasley. There's a chance Lucas is responsible somehow for these murders. At the least he incited that mob and cracked my skull. I aim to find him.'

'What will you do when you find him?'

'Why, hang him, of course.'

'Without proof?'

'Time I'm done with him he'll either confess or try to kill me. I won't need proof. Get inside, now. I thought I saw something over by the stable and I aim to take a look first.'

'I will not live in fear any longer,' she said, but turned and went into the house. Stopping in the doorway, she looked at him, a softness in her eyes now that the danger had passed. 'Be careful, Tom Hogan. Please.'

He nodded, reining around as she disappeared inside.

Dusk had deepened and the last shreds of twilight

painted the western sky with turquoise. Shadows reached from buildings and bunched near cottonwoods and evergreens. An orangey moon peeked above the horizon. Tom guided his bay towards the stable, dismounted. Drawing his Peacemaker, he kept a careful eye out for any threat. He had little wish to be surprised by whatever it was that had nearly attacked him on the trail the other night.

As he stepped into the stable, a horse whinnied and he jolted, despite himself. The gloom lay thicker in here and shadowy shapes of stalls and hay bales seemed exaggerated and somehow alien. He swung the Peacemaker in a protective arc.

'Anyone in here?' he called out, doubting he'd get an answer, but it gave him some sense of control.

He looked towards the horse who had made the noise, spotting nothing unusual, and the animal snorted. Likely it just wanted to be fed.

A shiver rode his spine and he realized he was plain boogered by the thought of running into something. He had never felt any particular fear of hardcases, but he was dealing with an unknown here. Was it Lucas Hasley? Or something else? Was it even human?

At the moment it didn't matter, because a search of the livery turned up nothing. Perhaps he had merely imagined seeing something. He had been in an agitated state and dusk made for tricks of vision.

He made his way outside, closed the stable doors and, holstering his gun, mounted. Riding around the grounds until darkness made seeing difficult, he found no sign of anything threatening. Still he couldn't quite shake the feeling something had been there. He debated going back to the house, but decided against it. Whatever was killing those doves in Wolf's Bend had

left Serene alone and there was little reason to think if
she stayed inside it wouldn't keep doing so.

Reining around, he gigged his horse in the direction
of town. He had an appointment with Lucas Hasley
and the hardcase was going to come clean and confess,
or go to his grave with the secret as far as Tom Hogan
was concerned.

Clinton Hasley stared out at the darkening street,
features cinched into grim lines. Anger simmered in
his belly as he watched seven men ride in, their faces
drained of the fever they had shown earlier when they
rode hell for leather towards the Hargrove place. They
had failed; that much was obvious. The reasons behind
it didn't matter. Lucas had ignored orders and his
blunder might cost them the whole operation. He
turned to look at his brother, who stood near the back,
arms folded, a blank look on his face.

'She's still there. It was too soon.' The words came
cold and damning, and Clinton's grey eyes glittered
with reproach. 'Your little mob wasn't ready enough. I
told you to wait. You should have let me work them
longer so there was no chance of failure. You're an
imbecile, Lucas. You have jeopardized the entire plan.'

The blank look on Lucas's face turned to annoyance.
'Don't talk to me that way, Clint. I don't like it.'

A flush of crimson heated Clinton's cheeks. 'I'll talk
to you any goddamn way I please.' His words came
through gritted teeth. He struggled to keep himself
from putting a bullet in Lucas. He needed to think fast,
before things fell apart completely and maybe that
manhunter sitting in the jail cell was the answer. 'We
best do something now. Go get rid of Hogan 'fore we got
even more trouble. Moon's coming up soon and maybe
if he appears to have died the same way as the others

we can still salvage this and work them up again.'

Lucas shifted feet, rubbed at his lower face.

'What's wrong?' Clinton's gaze narrowed behind his spectacles.

'Hell, we got another problem, Clint.'

Clinton's features went a shade darker and he took a step towards his brother. He knew even before Lucas said it that somehow Hogan had escaped. 'You simple-minded idiot!' His yell snapped like a whip. Anger made his heart pound in his ears and his fingers curl into fists. He considered getting the gun in the desk drawer and seeing to it Lucas never got a chance to ruin things again.

Cold fury jumped into Lucas's eyes. 'You got no gawddamn right callin' me that, Clint.' Spittle gathered at the corners of his mouth. Clinton saw no simpleton now, merely a vicious animal glare that convinced him his brother was far more lucid than he let on. Lucas took a step towards him and Clinton remained still. His brother was powerful, given to uncontrolled fits of temper that nearly always resulted in some brutal assault or a dead bargirl. If it had gotten worse and he was responsible for those torn-up doves, Clinton couldn't take any chances with him.

The point suddenly became moot. Lucas lunged, slamming into him with the force of a steam locomotive striking a buckboard. Clinton reeled backwards under the impact. He coughed out a sharp grunt as his back collided with the wall. Lucas endeavoured to get his beefy hands around Clinton's throat.

Using the same move he had tried on Hogan, Clinton knifed his arms upwards and outwards, snapping his brother's hold. He tried to jam a knee into Lucas's groin, but the hardcase was ready for that manoeuvre this time. He sidestepped, twisting his leg, and the knee struck his thigh. He lashed a hand across Clinton's face, raking four gory trenches deep into his flesh, and Clinton let out a yell of pain mixed with fury. Christ, his brother had killed those woman! That damn near proved it.

Clinton swung hard, a short chopping punch to Lucas's blocky jaw that sent him staggering back.

Making a dive for the wrench still on the table, Clinton intended to brain Lucas with it and end the threat permanently.

He didn't reach it. Lucas, feigning, wasn't as stunned as he appeared. He looped a punch that caught Clinton with stunning force across the temple. The newspaperman staggered, nearly losing control of his legs. His spectacles flew off and his senses spun. Another blow came directly after the first, crashing into his teeth, sending lances of pain across his jaw.

On instinct, he tried to swing back but was disoriented, off-balance, and missed.

Lucas snapped a violent kick that buried itself in Clinton's belly. Air burst from his lungs and lights exploded before his eyes. An uppercut followed that all but lifted him off the floor. All feeling deserting his legs, he went backward and down, thudding against the printing press, senses whirling.

After dragging moments, he stared up, eyes bleary, at the face of his brother, who hovered over him.

'You're gawddamn lucky I don't take a notion to kill you, Clint. But I appreciate what you done for me and blood is thicker than water, like they say. I'm done takin' your orders, though, and I'll get what's at the ranch myself, and take care of that Injun gal at the same time.'

Clinton could only gasp, mouth filled with the

gunmetal taste of his own blood. He watched, unable to move, as Lucas walked out the door.

Clinton remained that way for long moments, until fury rose and overcame the pain gripping his body. Pushing himself to his feet, he staggered to the back. He had planned too goddamn long to get hold of what was at that ranch house and he wasn't about to let that half-wit whore-killer brother of his ruin it for him, not now. If he acted fast enough he might catch Lucas before he reached the ranch. His brother would take the alternate route around the stream if he had any sense at all; he wouldn't want to risk encountering that manhunter along the trail. Clinton wouldn't either. But after he dealt with Lucas, Tom Hogan would have his killer and that woman would either leave or die.

After locating his spectacles, he went to a small desk and pulled open the drawer, taking out a gunbelt and strapping it on. He checked the Smith & Wesson for bullets, holstered it, then went out the back.

Darkness intensified by the time Tom Hogan reached Wolf's Bend. The moon had climbed halfway above the horizon, huge, orangey and mottled-looking. Hanging lanterns cast an eerie cider glow through the street and shadows seemed malevolent and reaching. Carousers were out in less force than usual. He reckoned that had something to do with Clinton Hasley's article and Lucas's rabble-rousing.

He reached the newspaper office, a sinking dread taking him at seeing the darkened window. By now surely the brothers had discovered his escape. Had they pulled stakes? He doubted it. Whatever they were after was enough to kill for and they would not abandon it so easily. A thought flashed through his mind: what if they had gone after Serene upon seeing their vigilantes fail? He forced the notion away. Certainly he would have encountered them on the trail if that were the case.

Reining up and dismounting, he drew his gun and edged on to the boardwalk.

Trying the door, he found it unlocked and the dread stepped up a notch. He eased it open, stepped inside, gaze shifting left and right, the Peacemaker following the same path. The office appeared deserted.

Where the hell had they gone?

'They headed out,' a voice came from behind him and he whirled, drawing a bead on the dark figure silhouetted in the doorway.

'You scared the hell out of me, boy!' Tom lowered his Peacemaker.

Clay Hargrove stepped into the office. 'Didn't rightly mean to, but I saw you ride in and figured you'd come to make Hasley pay for what he done to you. You stop them vigilantes?'

'They didn't take much persuadin'. Reckon Lucas didn't work 'em long enough to make it stick.'

Clay nodded. 'Glad it worked out that way.'

'Thought you did your penance and was ridin' out?'

Clay shrugged. 'I got to thinkin' I still had some more repentin' to do. I figured if you didn't come back it might come down to me havin' to avenge Miss Serene.'

'That's right thinkin', but it ain't necessary any longer.'

'Might be. I saw Lucas tear out of here like holy hell and head for the livery for a horse. He rode off towards the east. Not too long after his brother followed.'

Tom cocked an eyebrow. 'The east? Stream's in that direction.'

Clay nodded. 'So is the old trail that leads in a

round-about way to the Hargrove ranch. It's longer, but smoother and sometimes me and Jothan led horses that way to work them out a bit after they'd been shipped in and we fetched them at the livery.'

Tom sighed. 'Makes sense they'd go that way. Reckon they discovered I'd gotten out and they didn't want to run into me on the trail, considering the frame of mind they put me in.'

'They got a good head start, but reckon we can catch them.'

Tom peered at Clay Hargrove, seeing new courage shine in the boy's eyes. But this time there were only two men and Tom could handle that better alone. Clay would be an unknown in a confrontation with the Hasleys and he couldn't be sure how the younger man would react. Any miscalculation or slight slip might prove fatal for Serene, as it had for that woman twenty years ago. He couldn't take that risk.

'You've paid your debt, boy. Ain't no need to make a life's work of it. Get out of here and don't look back. Don't fret over anything any more. I can handle the Hasleys better by myself. I work better that way and that's Serene's best chance.'

'What about that killer?'

'Reckon they might be one and the same. Lucas Hasley showed me that when he raked my face. He's capable of doin' what happened to them doves.'

Clay gave a short nod. 'Much obliged, Mr Hogan, but I think I'll stick around. Miss Serene might need help runnin' that ranch if things work out OK.'

A thin smile turned his lips. 'She might at that. Things don't work out you ride as far and as fast from here as you can. Ain't no need to waste your life paying for imagined sins.'

The notion struck him he was a first class hypocrite,

and not one to be dolin' out that kind of advice, but maybe it was simple realization taking hold. He hoped Clay Hargrove took his advice and didn't make the mistake a young manhunter had, but sometimes youth paid no nevermind. He knew that only too well.

He pushed past the boy and went to his horse. The Hasleys were likely converging on the ranch at this very moment and he had little time to stop them. Reining around, he let out a sharp 'Yah!' and heeled his horse into a gallop, tearing through the main street and riding into the rising moon.

NINE

Lucas Hasley dismounted and tethered his horse to a tree at the edge of the Hargrove property. His gaze swept across the moon- and shadow-streaked grounds. He rubbed a hand across his blocky chin. Things looked different, vaguely forbidding in the moonlight. He had ridden close to the spread a few times before, but always during the day. Starin' at the place for hours, he would try to figure out where old Hargrove might have hidden that stuff.

He wondered if that Injun woman might have found it, but quickly discounted the possibility. He reckoned if she had discovered the secret she wouldn't have been running this ranch by herself. He had spotted the 'breed tending to chores or the horses plenty of times, and she was downright pretty for a squaw. He had considered takin' her and wagered she'd be right fine in the hay. Only the thought of them Injun spirits – and Clint's reaction – had held him back.

But now he wasn't going to let Injun ghosts or Clint get in his way. 'Sides, he knew all along no Injun hoodoo had killed them gals in town. But he wasn't so sure about them fellers and Lulu Belle; somethin' had shore torn the livin' hell outta them. He had his

138

notions Clint might know more 'bout that than he was tellin', but somethin' about it didn't quite cipher. Why would Clint kill Hargrove before he got the location? And why would his brother murder his own man or that crooked lawdog?

Lucas gave up pondering it. Thinkin' wasn't exactly his strong suit. Till now, Clint had done most of the thinkin', but Lucas was sick and whole-hog tired of takin' Clint's orders. Old Clint's way wasn't doin' them a lick of good and his brother was gawddamn lucky Lucas hadn't just decided to beat his brains out for talkin' to him the way he did. Hell, it made no nevermind. Once he got what Hargrove hid on this spread he could find another town and buy all the gals and whiskey he wanted, without Clint tellin' him what to do.

He let out a laugh, thinking about the look on Clint's face once he found out his dimdot kin had ridden off with Hargrove's secret. Old Lucas wasn't as slow as his brother thought. That arrowhead in his brain hadn't slowed his think box at all, he reckoned. He jest let Clint and other folks figure as much because it suited his purpose. Nobody paid much nevermind to a simpleton.

A blank look crossed Lucas's eyes. His gristly forehead knotted. For a moment he stared off into the darkness and the world swirled with a strange purplish mist. A whoop echoed from the depths of his memory and the Apache warrior stepped from the violet haze, aiming an arrow and drawing back—

He let out a grunt as a twinge of pain stabbed through his brain, snapping him back to the present. Focusing again on the moonbathed grounds, he shook his head and rubbed his temple. Hell, he hated recollectin' that. Clint hadn't known he'd killed that brave's

squaw and that was why the Injun put an arrow
through his skull.

Lucas edged closer to the grounds, pausing, wondering where he should start. A thin mist slithered in,
glazed with moonglow.

Where would Hargrove have hidden it?

Lucas's gaze settled on the darkened stable, eyes
narrowing. Hargrove had a thing for fine horses, spent
lots of time with 'em, Clinton had told him. Made sense
he might hide it in there. Lucas thought it over. He
reckoned that was the most likely place but the
thought of searchin' around in that darkened building
gave him pause. Hargrove had died in that stable.
What if them Injun spirits lived in there?

The front door of the ranch-house opened, pulling
him from his thoughts. He shrank back behind a
cottonwood. Tensing, he watched as the woman
stepped out on to the porch, a Winchester in her hand.

She paused at the edge of the porch, looking out at
the moonlit night. He saw her Injun features plainly in
the alabaster glow. He considered going after her,
taking care of her right away, havin' a little fun with
her first. But she held a rifle and he was unarmed. He
didn't need guns to do what needed doin'. Beatin' up
whores felt a whole lot more satisfyin' than shootin'
them.

As she stepped off the porch and headed in the
direction of the stream, he let her go. He could deal
with her later. Right now Hargrove's stuff was more
important and with her out of the way he was free to
search for it without worry.

Eyeing the stable, he suppressed a momentary
ripple of unease.

'Injun spirits, hell!' he told himself.

He crept to the stable in a crouch. The doors were

closed. He eased the beam up and pushed them open, letting in as much illumination as possible.

A howl rose in the night and he damn near pissed his britches. With a sharp breath he cursed them damn prairie wolves for boogering him such.

He stepped into the stable and gloom engulfed him. A horse nickered to his left.

'Shut the hell up!' he snapped at the animal, banging a fist against the stall door.

The stable was marbled in onyx and opal. The thready mist wandered through the doors, slinking over the hay-strewn floor. He spotted stalls and hay bales, a pitchfork leaning against a supporting beam. Taking slow breaths, he studied each corner. If Hargrove hid it in here, where would it be?

. He recollected Clint sayin' Hargrove had built this place soon after arriving in Wolf's Bend. What if he had built something into it, maybe the floor or a wall, some sort of storage space?

Going deeper into the stable, he stamped lightly, listening to the ring of his bootheel on the floorboards. Every plank sounded solid and a prickle of mild annoyance took him.

He paused, scratching his head, wondering if he were mistaken.

'Christamighty, nuthin' . . .' he mumbled.

A sound.

Low and ominous, a growl, like that of some sort of animal. Except it didn't quite sound like no animal he'd ever heared. It was too throaty.

A chill trickled down his spine and for the first time he could recollect he felt downright scared. Hell, maybe it was jest all them stories about full moons and Injun hoodoos gettin' to him.

Tarnation, maybe he should jest go get Clint. That

way there'd be two of 'em and if those Injun' spirits killed anyone it would be his brother.

He shook his head. No, he didn't need Clint and wasn't going to share what Hargrove had stashed with anyone.

He took another couple steps forward, muscles tight, trying to figure out where the growl had come from.

A horse shuffled nervously in its stall, snorting and that just made Lucas's nerves sing all the worse.

'Gawddamn glue . . .'

Another sound.

This one was far different and stopped him in his tracks. A scraping noise of some sort—

'Judas Priest!' he whispered, almost a gasp. Just ahead of him a portion of the floor began to rise with an eerie creaking. Strands of hay fell away as a hatch in the floor opened and he knew he had guessed right – Hargrove had built a secret place into the stable.

Hell, wouldn't Old Clint just piss his britches when he found out his half-wit brother had discovered where—

Wait.

That door wasn't coming up by its lonesome and that was a gawddamn problem. Whatever was lifting it was likely responsible for that growl and he recollected hearin' some of them Injun spirits lived in the ground and—

'Christ on a crutch!' He lurched backward as he caught a glimpse of the fearsome dark shape rising from the floor. The hatch flew backward with a violent sweep of the thing's clawed hand and landed with a shuddery crash against the floorboards. A monstrous figure leaped from the hole, hulking and shadowy, its great furred wolf's head silhouetted in a halo of moonlight, huge clawed hands slashing the air. It poised on the edge of the hole in a crouch, issuing a low growl that sent ripples of fear down his spine.

Locas stared at it, frozen. It was the biggest gawd-damn Injun spirit he'd ever laid eyes on, at least three inches taller than his own six-foot-two frame. Dark and covered with fur, its elongated features were indistinguishable in the gloom.

'What the hell are you?' he yelled, suddenly whirling and making a maddened dash for the stable doors.

The thing pounced before he could get outside. It slammed into him with the force of a charging long-horn and Lucas Hasley knew he had just encountered something incredibly powerful.

He hit the ground hard, air punched from his lungs in an explosive gasp. A scream tore from his throat. Twisting, the last thing he saw was a great claw slashing towards his neck; then he felt his lifeblood spouting from his torn-out Adam's apple. As blackness engulfed his senses he swore he heard a howl filling the stable and fading into eternal damnation.

Standing by the parlour window, peering out into the encroaching night, Serene Hargrove let out a heavy sigh and wished she did not feel so helpless. Tom Hogan had left nearly an hour ago to ride into town and confront Lucas Hasley. A gnawing unease made her wonder if he had met with some sort of mishap. Lucas Hasley from all accounts was a violent man, and if he were responsible for those murders . . .

Her worry strengthened, whispering like night spirits in her heart. She eyed the Winchester resting on the rack and wondered if she should ride into Wolf's Bend and look for him.

He had told her to stay in the house, lock the doors. But that made little sense with the Hasleys in town, or if they had killed Tom. Had Lucas Hasley murdered Jothan and those other men? Had he killed those bargirls? Tom seemed to think so, though she saw doubts in his eyes, the same doubts that had occurred to her. Why would Lucas kill his own brother's messenger? Perhaps there were reasons she or Tom did not suspect. Perhaps a man such as he needed no logic or motive other than sheer viciousness.

It did not matter.

Her decision was made. She went to the rifle, lifting it from the rack. She would not wait for death to come. She had cowered in fear countless nights, dreading Jothan's return, his cruelness, and this felt the same. She would give Tom Hogan another hour, then go to Wolf's Bend to search for him. In the meantime she refused to remain in this house a moment longer.

Going to the door, she stepped out on to the porch. Her gaze swept across the moonlit vista and she saw nothing moving, no sign of threat. She had never feared the night and would not start now.

Crossing the porch, she paused, went down the stairs and across the yard, letting the breeze flow over her. A pleasant chill touched the air and a satiny mist moved over the ground, embedded with sparkling jewels of moonglow. On most nights it would have calmed her, provided her strength and solace. But not tonight. Tonight she had too much at stake.

She walked towards the stream, praying time would flow fast and she would hear his horse's hoofbeats any moment.

A howl came and she knew coyote was near. She smiled, relaxing a little.

Reaching the stream, she stared out for a moment at the water tumbling along, glassy streaks of liquid light rushing over the rocks and gently singing to her. She began a low chant for victory and hope, while she waited for coyote to come to her. The animal was her guide, her reminder of strength. He had taught her much, especially about affection given with little asked in return.

A noise caught her attention and she turned, expecting to see the animal behind her, eager for scraps of food or companionship.

The thin smile fell from her lips. Her heart leaped into her throat when she saw a dark figure standing behind her, a menacing expression on his hard features.

'Well, well, Mrs Hargrove, I see Lucas somehow managed to foul up even killing you the way he threatened – or did you do away with him?' Clinton Hasley held a Smith & Wesson aimed at her chest.

She glared at him, wondering if she could get her rifle up in time but judging she could not. 'I have not seen your brother, Mr Hasley. He has no business here.'

Moonlight glinted off his spectacles. 'Well, I'm inclined to agree there, Mrs Hargrove. But I *do* have business here. See, your husband left a legacy you know nothing about and I aim to have it.'

A growl came from Hasley's right and the newspaperman's head swivelled. Serene's gaze went to the animal who had appeared at the edge of the brush. The coyote's eyes glinted with intent at the man who posed a threat to its human companion. Its ears were pulled back, the hair standing up along its spine. She knew it would protect her but Hasley had a gun; the beast would be no match for that.

'Coyote, go!' she snapped, urgency in her voice.

'Goddamn mangy thing!' Hasley shouted, swinging the Smith & Wesson around. 'That how you killed your husband?'

Serene leaped at him, heedless of her own safety. She tried to bring the butt of the Winchester up in the same motion, intending to strike the newspaperman before he could fire.

Hasley was too fast. He triggered a shot just as the coyote whirled and bolted at her command. The coyote yelped as lead tore a streak across its left haunch, but didn't lose stride. It plunged into the brush, vanishing.

Hasley, no time for a second shot, let out a curse and spun, backhanding Serene just as she brought the rifle up. His blow took her full in the mouth and pain vibrated through her teeth. Legs going out from beneath her, she went backwards and down, the Winchester flying from her grip.

She sat up, fury tightening her features. She had sworn no man would ever do that to her again. 'Do not strike me again, Mr Hasley or I will kill you.'

Hasley bellowed a laugh. 'Don't seem to me you're in much of a position to be making threats. Get up, Mrs Hargrove. You and me are gonna make a little stop at your house to get us a lantern and start lookin' over this spread for what your husband left.' He paused, face hardening. 'Then we're gonna find that no good brother of mine and see if the coyote killer doesn't need itself a couple more victims 'fore it disappears.'

TEN

Tom Hogan slowed his bay as he reached the end of the trail. His heart beat thick in his throat and anxiousness made his nerves sing. Scanning the compound, he noted the house was alight and everything seemed tranquil. But a simmering dread told him that meant nothing. He could not have arrived before the Hasleys. Although he spotted no sign of Lucas or Clinton, he knew they were here, somewhere. In all likelihood Lucas Hasley was a brutal killer, though Tom had nagging doubts about the hardcase's total guilt in the game. Whatever Tom had glimpsed on the trail the other night was big enough to be Lucas, yet the stalker appeared more animal-like than human. Still, he hadn't gotten a clean look at the thing. And unless Lucas was working against his brother, he had no reason to kill a messenger or the sheriff, or even Lulu Belle as far as Tom could see.

He urged his horse forward at a cautious gait, eyes wary, shifting left then right for any sign of trouble. Fifty yards on he reined up and dismounted, tethering his horse to a tree branch.

A howl rose in the night, sending a shiver down his

spine. The moon glazed the mist with an eerie glow. Shadows shifted into menacing shapes.

A snort to his left caught his attention and he made out the shape of another horse secured to a branch. That had to be one of the Hasley mounts, but which one?

A terror-filled shriek jolted him and his gun flashed into his hand. With a measure of relief he noted the cry didn't belong to a woman. He paused, listening, gun heavy in his grip. Whoever had made that scream likely had taken his last breath.

It's in there . . .

His gaze settled on the looming moon-glazed outline of the stable. The doors gaped open like a black maw. He started forward, alert, half crouched.

Christ, Hogan, you sure you really want to meet up with whatever caused a man to cry out that way?

Tom let out a stuttering breath. He reached the stable, hand tightening on the Peacemaker.

A sudden whooping howl came from the interior, freezing him where he stood. The same howl he heard the other night, not coyote, but something . . .

Human?

He wasn't sure. A sinking notion told him it sure as hell wasn't Lucas or Clinton Hasley. The dying scream he had heard a moment ago held a mighty familiar ring to it.

'Come on out of there!' he yelled, angling just off to the side so he'd be protected by the wall in case a bullet answered.

A hushed silence fell and he heard his heart thudding. Sweat trickled down his chest and he ran his tongue over dry lips.

It's in there, Hogan and it ain't comin' out. You're gonna have to go in after it. . .

Hell.

He eased around the corner of the door. Moonlight outlined the interior and he saw no hint of movement, heard nothing.

He moved inside and suddenly his boot toe encountered something spongy and he looked down.

'Jesus H. Christmas . . .' he muttered. The shredded deathmask of Lucas Hasley shone ghastly in a puddle of moonlight, eyes glazed, staring sightlessly in frozen terror. Any theory of Hasley being the murderer seemed suddenly moot.

A swish sounded to his side. From the corner of his eye he caught a flash of dark movement and instinctively dove forward. The move undoubtedly saved his life, but he took a glancing blow to the temple that sent a curtain of stars sparkling across his vision. He slammed into the floor with stunning force. The Peacemaker jolted from his grip, skittering off in the darkness. Dazed, he rolled and came up in a crouch, but was off-balance.

A shadowy form came out of the darkness. Surrounded by an aura of moonlight, the thing appeared huge, monstrous, the great furred head of an animal atop the body of a man. Huge hairy hands, claws glinting with moonlight, told him what had ripped Hasley apart. The creature – for that's all he could label it – powerful legs uncoiling, catapulted itself through the air like a mountain lion springing from a ledge.

Tom threw himself sideways. His position was awkward and he mistimed the move, but the creature missed him.

Frightened, horses shuffled about in their stalls, let out nervous snorts and whinnies.

Tom struggled to regain his balance, glancing up

and getting a bead on the creature before it launched another attack.

The creature had landed on its feet a few yards away. It moved with remarkable swiftness for all its huge size, closing the distance in seconds.

Tom, half-standing, tried to go to his right, but the beast compensated instantly and shifted with him, lashing out with a hairy hand.

Pain skewered his belly as the claws shredded his shirt and tore gory welts across his abdomen. The cuts weren't deep but they stung like hell, bled liberally. He was lucky the thing hadn't gutted him. He staggered sideways, gaze locked on the attacker.

The creature, growling, came forward again.

Tom set his balance. Swivelling on a heel, he launched a side kick that caught the thing square in the chest. The blow connected with a heavy thud and the impact hurled the beast backward a half dozen steps, but did little else. The attacker was powerful.

Tom's breath beat out hot and ragged. Gaze roving, he tried to spot where his Peacemaker had landed. If he didn't recover the piece he would stand little chance against the creature. It had the advantage of strength and speed and razor-sharp talons, and was all too at home in the semi-darkness.

The creature shifted left. Tom backed along the stalls, struggling to catch his breath.

The thing sprang without warning and he snapped a reflexive punch at its elongated head. The blow was hurried and the attacker jerked its hairy skull out of the way. His fist bounced off its furry shoulder, doing no damage.

A claw looped in a roundhouse slash that caught him a glancing blow as he tried to duck under it. It ricocheted off his head just behind the ear and hurled him sideways. He stumbled, barely retaining his legs. His senses reeled and everything streaked by, a blur of shadow and vanilla haze.

He kept his legs but, dazed, had no chance to recover or defend himself. The creature caught him, hoisted him off the ground and flung him backwards. He crashed into a stall, crumpling to the ground on hands and knees. Blackness swirled in from the corners of his mind. He struggled to his feet, drawing gasping breaths.

The stable interior suddenly grew lighter and Tom was vaguely aware of someone at the entrance. He caught the sound of a woman's gasp, and knew it was Serene, but couldn't look towards her. The second he did the thing in front of him would tear out his throat.

The creature hesitated with the light, glancing towards the doorway, then back at Tom. Tom got a clear look at it then. It was a man, but he was wearing some sort of headdress made from the top part of a preserved wolf's head. A pelt covered his shoulders, laced to his form with rawhide about the neck and beneath the arms. Hairy hide gloves with talons sewn in to the fingertips were fastened with leather strips to either of the man's hands; wolf's hair boots reached his knees. He wore little else, his chest bare, streaked with black body paint, and a breech clout reached to mid-thigh. He was large, muscles bulging from his arms and thighs. A rank musky odour of hide and unwashed skin assailed Tom's nostrils.

The beast-man lunged at Tom, intent on finishing him off. A great furred hand slashed at his throat.

Tom dived sideways and the claw thunked into the stall door. Splinters tore from the wood as the attacker yanked his talons free. Tom took advantage of the split second chance and snapped another kick into his assailant's ribs, hearing one crack. The man-beast staggered slightly, grunted, but otherwise seemed unaffected. He spun towards Tom.

Gasping, strength deserting him, Tom fell back against a stall. He had no chance against the killer unless he found his gun or some other equalizer.

Gaze snapping left and right, he searched for a weapon. A pitchfork rested against a supporting beam a few feet away. He had a slim chance at reaching it. If he failed . . .

The man-beast must have guessed his intent because he lunged. Tom grabbed for the pitchfork just as claws raked his back, tearing shreds from his shirt and gouging deep trenches into his flesh. With a grunt of pain, he staggered, the makeshift weapon just out of reach. He wouldn't make it. The attacker had him and one more swipe would bring death.

Serene screamed and the man-beast hesitated, swinging its head in her direction.

Tom stumbled sideways, taking advantage of his attacker's indecision. Making a final desperate attempt for the pitchfork, he got his hands around the handle, jerked it towards him. He let out a yell, whirling, sweeping it up in a short powerful arc.

The attacker's head jerked around. He let out a whooping howl, threw himself at Tom, lashing out with a taloned hand that streaked towards the manhunter's throat.

Tom thrust the pitchfork forward with all his remaining strength. A sickening crunch sounded as the tines penetrated flesh and muscle.

He let go, shoving the man-beast backward. The attacker clutched at his belly, trying to pull the pitchfork loose. Blood bubbled from around the tines, ran over the furred hands. He staggered backwards, went down hard on his back. The pitchfork tore free and fell to the side. The body twitched, went still.

Tom collapsed against the stall, panting. His gaze lifted to the entrance. Serene stood in the doorway, holding a lantern before her, tears running from her eyes, utter horror on her face. Clinton Hasley stood behind her, an arm locked around her neck and a Smith & Wesson jammed to her temple.

'Congratulations, Mr Hogan.' Clinton Hasley's voice was mocking, hard. He forced Serene into the stable a half dozen steps. 'You got our killer.' He glanced at the body of Lucas and laughed. 'And our killer got Lucas. How appropriate.' He nudged his head towards the fallen man-creature. 'Go ahead, take off that wolf mask and see who's underneath. Reckon it's as much a mystery to me as it is to you.'

Tom glanced at Serene, then went to the creature. Kneeling, he lifted the wolf's head from the man's face and black hair tumbled out. The man's dark eyes stared sightlessly ahead. Tom shook his head and straightened.

Hasley's face lit with surprise. 'I'll be, an Injun. Guess Lucas was right about them after all.'

'He is Striking Wolf.' Serene's voice came brittle and low. Shock and horror played on her face.

Tom understood now. The man she'd been promised to had found her, protected her by killing anyone he decided posed a threat. It was Striking Wolf Tom had glimpsed on the trail, dressed in the wolf getup, not Lucas Hasley. He felt regret rise at having ended the man's life, though surely the Apache would have taken his.

He looked at Hasley, eyes narrowing. 'This man might have killed Serene's husband and those two other men, but he had no reason to kill whores in town.'

'I'm afraid you're right about that, Mr Hogan. You can blame those killings on poor Lucas, here. See, Lucas liked to beat his women rather extensively. Appears some of them didn't survive. I misjudged him, though. Apparently he wasn't quite the simpleton I thought because I reckon he started tearin' them up to blame it on a convenient killer. I am amazed he thought of it.'

'Why'd he kill Lulu Belle if she was helpin' him and you with doves?'

'I must admit the responsibility for that one is mine, Mr Hogan. And it pains me to say Lucas thought of blaming that killer a step ahead of me.'

'You killed her? Why, Hasley? She did you favours?'

'Lulu Belle got greedy, Mr Hogan. You see, she was one of Jothan Hargrove's favourite gals. He started confidin' in her about something hidden out here at the ranch because he needed help with it. She suggested me. He sent her to me with a proposition, which I accepted. That should have been all there was to it, but for some inane reason she decided I had killed Hargrove and tried to blackmail me by threatening to tell the town that and that I was with her. I assure you it would have been a sticky situation and I couldn't have it jeopardizing my plans. Funny thing is I couldn't kill Hargrove because he wouldn't tell me where the stuff was hidden and frankly I might have been satisfied with half the profits if the extent of what he said he had was true.'

Tom wiped a dribble of blood from his lips. 'So you caught her comin' out of the hotel that night and dragged her to the alley after ripping her to pieces?'

Hasley's face took on a look of gloating. His grey eyes sparkled with some sort of perverted glee. 'Not exactly, Mr Hogan. I had arranged a meeting with her, told her I was going to give her her first payment. She showed up and I killed her in back of the print shop, then snuck her body in back of the saloon before meeting with you. It's truly amazing what a piece of barbed wire will do to a whore's body . . .'

Tom knew he had to stall for time. His gaze darted, searching for his Peacemaker, spotting it lying about twenty feet away.

His eyes locked on the newspaperman. 'What did Hargrove have out here you wanted, Hasley?'

Hasley's gaze shifted and Tom glanced backwards, seeing an open trapdoor in the stable floor. The newspaperman prodded Serene deeper in the stable, manoeuvring around until Tom was backed near the opening. 'Shine the lantern down there, Mrs Hargrove,' he ordered, pressing the gun harder into her temple. She gasped but held out the light. The lantern glow illuminated a cubicle roughly seven feet square. Inside were scattered scraps of food, which Striking Wolf must have stolen for the times he concealed himself within the cubby. Likely he had seen Hargrove open it at some point.

A number of strong boxes were stacked along two walls, along with canvas bags from banks.

Hasley grinned, obviously pleased with what he saw. He manoeuvred Serene back towards the stable doorway and Tom sweated every inch.

Tom's mind raced. This time he had to think of something, use his experience and reverse the results of twenty years ago. But circumstances were worse this time. He had no gun and Hasley could not afford to let either of them walk out of the stable alive. 'What's in the boxes? Hargrove tell you?'

'Oh, he told me, just didn't tell me where it was. You see, when he came to Wolf's Bend, Hargrove set himself up right nicely. Just wandered in one day and started throwin' all sorts of money around, hiring builders to get this place up faster than all get out. Built himself a stable and got some fine horses and a squaw, too.'

'Where'd the money come from?'

'Hargrove told me he was the inside man for the Red Widow Gang that famous manhunter Luke Banner brought down right before he died. Everyone thought that gang all perished the day they tried to rob some stage after Banner set them up. He got himself killed when he went after the leader, but he must have found out someone was feeding the gang information about the stages 'cause lawdogs started crawlin' around Zellers Stage Lines looking for the informant. Hargrove pulled stakes faster than a squirrel eyein' a squaw with a stew pot. Law never found most of the gold and jewels and cash the gang made off with. Hargrove knew where it was and liberated it.'

'Why did he need you?'

'He didn't know how to get rid of the jewels and gold. He went through the cash quicker than he went through his rotgut and was startin' to get in a bind with some creditors over horseflesh. Lulu Belle knew I could turn it into cash. I wanted half but Hargrove was haggling with me over it for a more than a month. I figured I could outlast him. Sooner or later he'd have to settle on my terms or lose his ranch to creditors. That's what's in the boxes, Mr Hogan, the swag from the Red Widow Gang and I won't have any problem disposing of it. Won't have to share it now, either, with Hargrove *or* Lucas.'

Tom raised an eyebrow. 'So you kill us and just take it?'

'That's the plan, Hogan. Reckon that killer made

disposing of you two mighty convenient and I will of course be mourning the loss of a brother.'

A growl sounded behind Hasley and the man jolted. Tom tensed, seeing the newspaperman's eyes shift and turn his head to look behind him.

A form leaped out of the darkness beyond the entrance, lips curled back from vicious teeth. Serene's coyote! The animal sailed through the air straight for Clinton Hasley and he panicked.

Serene dropped straight down at the same instant.

Hasley tried to keep hold of her but she jerked away and the lantern went flying from her grip. It smashed with an explosive *whoof!* against a stall and flames sprang across the wood.

Hasley couldn't get this gun around in time and the coyote landed on his shoulders, jaws snapping at the man's throat. He gyrated madly, struggling to throw off the beast or get his pistol up to kill it.

Tom wasted no time. He leaped for his gun, diving and grabbing it, momentum carrying him over in a somersault. He came up in a crouch.

Flames leaped across the stalls, devouring dry wood and crisping stands of hay. Black smoke billowed out.

Serene screamed as Hasley got his gun into the coyote's side.

Tom lifted his Peacemaker in a fluid blur of motion. This time his hand was steady, his aim true. His finger feathered the trigger and a shot blasted.

The impact kicked Hasley backwards before he could put a bullet into the coyote. The beast flew sideways, landing on its feet, and scurried towards Serene.

'Coyote, go!' she snapped and the creature hesitated, its brow knotted, dark eyes appearing worried. 'Go, I'll be OK,' she said and the coyote whirled and fled.

Hasley gyrated, trying to get his gun back up,

though a blotch of scarlet ripened across his front. The
man was alive by pure force of evil will.

Grim determination on his face, Tom straightened,
calmly triggering another shot. The bullet punched
into Hasley's breastbone.

The newspaperman dropped, a startled, unbelieving
expression flooding his grey eyes. He fell face first,
spectacles flying off and shattering.

The heat grew intense. Smoke stung Tom's eyes,
choked his lungs. A few feet away Serene was coughing, gasping. Horses neighed in terror, kicking at stall
doors with thunderous crashes.

Tom holstered his gun and turned to Serene. She
was throwing open one of the stall doors and yelling at
the horse to run. The sorrel bolted and she ran to the
next.

Tom rushed to the stalls on the right, hurling open
doors, shouting. Sweat streamed in dirty streaks down
his face. He was gasping, barely able to breath.

Flames roared, crackled, streaked up walls and
supporting beams, which groaned, threatening to
collapse.

'Serene, get out! The whole place is gonna come
down.'

She got the last horse out and he finished his side,
sending the terrified animals into the night. They
could round them up later.

A beam tore from the ceiling and crashed down with
an explosion of sparks. Strength failing, he staggered
to Serene as she slumped, gasping and coughing,
against a stall. Grabbing her arm, he pulled her
towards the door. She started to fall and he caught her,
getting both arms beneath hers and dragging her out
into the crisp night air.

Behind them flames roared up and swallowed the

stable. Beams came crashing down and clouds of smoke and sparks billowed into the night.

At the edge of the property the coyote howled a mournful howl.

Three weeks passed and Tom Hogan reckoned he had finally freed the wolf inside him. Standing in the small cemetery at the edge of town, head hung low as he stared at a simple marker which bore the name Bretina Winslow, he felt a sense of melancholy ride through him. But this time it was the feeling of something finished, something that had gone on for too long, died a lingering death. He reckoned it would still take time before the nightmares ended, if in fact they ever did, but Serene would help him through that and he would help her through hers. They had a lifetime to work on it.

As soon as the remains of the stable cooled, they had dug out the strong boxes and returned the loot to Zellers Stage Lines for accounting. They'd received a small reward, enough to keep the ranch going for a spell, but she wouldn't need that because he had enough money from manhunting for them to live on comfortably and he'd asked her to marry him. She quickly agreed and he'd told her he would give up his profession and make a go of the ranch. Clay had come back to help.

He kneeled, placing a rose on the grave, taking a slow breath. 'Reckon I made a mistake twenty years ago, ma'am,' he whispered. 'I hope I've atoned for it now and you'll find it in your heart to forgive me, wherever you are.'

He straightened, emotion choking his throat, the man he had been for twenty years dying, following that woman he'd failed to save all those years ago to the grave.

A hand touched his shoulder and he turned to see Serene gazing sympathetically at him, dark eyes kind and compassionate. She was everything he could ever ask for in a life he had spent far too much time wasting.

She took his arm and they walked from the cemetery towards his horse. A strange sense of calmness filled him and somewhere in the distant darkness of his mind a wolf howled for the very last time.